# The Diva's Bodyguard

Sweet Country Music Romance, Book 2

## Penelope Spark

I0543245

# 1

Maggie Hammer sat on her new leather couch, staring down at the letter trembling in her hand. She'd read it a hundred times, but still, she couldn't stop looking at it. The signature, which wasn't much of a signature at all, was smudged from an accidental tear splash the day before. Before the smear, it had read, "Your Fan." Except that this guy was no fan.

This was the third letter she'd received and it was the scariest. She'd posted the help-wanted ad after receiving the second letter. A few interested parties had inquired, but when she'd stated the salary, those parties had quickly lost interest. One candidate hadn't asked about pay, and he was due for an interview in ten minutes. Dane Longley.

Her leg bounced up and down as she waited for him to arrive. She'd thought about interviewing him somewhere other than her living room, but she didn't want to go out in public without a bodyguard. *There's security at the gate*, she reminded herself. She'd given them Dane's name. This was going to be fine. Perfectly safe.

The doorbell rang, and she jumped. He was early. That was a good sign—probably. She stood, smoothed out her short skirt, and headed for the door. What she saw when she opened it took her breath away. The man was huge. His arms looked like tree trunks. She knew that most bodyguards were muscular, but this guy went beyond the stereotype.

She already felt safer. She stepped back and waved her hand toward her foyer. "Please, come in." As he walked by her, she caught a familiar scent. It was wonderful, but it took her a second to place it. Then it came to her. He smelled like a fir tree, like a Christmas tree. And though she wasn't a fan of Christmas exactly, the smell gave her an odd sense of peace.

He stepped into her living room and looked around. "Nice place." His voice was deep and gravelly.

She wondered what his singing voice would sound like. "Thanks. Please, have a seat." She pointed toward the chair facing her sofa, which she returned to.

Looking tentative, he perched on the edge of the chair and rested his elbows on his knees. Was he always this alert?

She crossed her long, bare legs and flashed him a saucy smile she hoped would charm him into working for minimum wage. "Thank you for coming on such short notice. I have found myself in a situation."

He nodded. "Happy to help."

She picked up his cover letter and resume, which he had emailed beforehand, from her coffee table. "I called your references, of course, and they speak very highly of you." She glanced up at him.

As she expected, he looked uncomfortable.

She looked at his resume again. "But I can't help wondering why you didn't list Kate Leece as a reference?" According to his resume, she was his most recent employer, his only non-military employer, and his only previous bodyguard experience.

He smoothed out his black slacks and exhaled slowly. "Can I be honest?"

"I would prefer it."

He grinned, and when he did, his eyes sparkled.

She didn't like that one bit. She didn't have time to be distracted by anyone's sparkly anything, especially not someone who was going to be working for her day in and day out.

"There was an incident. I messed up. Kate fired me."

The man certainly liked to speak in short sentences. "I see." She didn't really. Not yet. "What kind of incident?"

He averted her gaze and stared at an empty wall. "I saw a threat where there wasn't one." He didn't elaborate.

"Can you tell me more?" She failed to keep the impatience out of her voice.

He looked at her then, and the intensity of his gaze unnerved her. "There was an overly aggressive fan. I thought he was a threat. So I neutralized him."

*What?* "You neutralized him? What does that mean?" He hadn't murdered a fan, had he?

"I mean, I made sure he wasn't a threat." He rolled his eyes then, at himself, apparently, and leaned back in the chair, dropping his big hands onto the armrests. "I hit him. I hit him once, and he hit the pavement. The ambulance came. Now she's paying for his medical bills and no longer paying me."

Maggie wasn't sure what to say.

He started to get up. "Sorry for wasting your time."

Wait, what was he doing? She grabbed for his arm. "No, no, please ... stay."

He looked down at her with obvious surprise in his eyes.

She slowly removed her hand from his arm, scrambling to think of something to say, some rational reason why she might be willing to overlook an assault and a firing. Some reason other than he was the only one who had applied for the job. "I'd rather have someone who overreacts than someone who under-reacts. I'm not just hiring a bodyguard because that's something celebrities do. I have a real threat."

He sat down abruptly, his brow furrowed. "Tell me."

# 2

Dane could see fear in her eyes. She was trying to hide it, but it was there. He tried to focus on that curiosity instead of on his own guilt. He hadn't told her everything, not even close. But he should. He should be honest. Without his integrity, who was he?

Who was he? Broke. That's who he was. He needed this job.

"Have you heard about me?" she asked in a mousy voice unlike the one she'd used thus far. "I mean, you know about my family?"

He nodded. Of course he did. The whole world knew. "I know you left your family's band to go solo. Is that what you mean?"

She nodded quickly. "And it got pretty ugly. My mom is not happy."

"So you need someone to protect you from your mother?" He was kidding, mostly, but she didn't laugh. What did he know? Maybe she really did have a crazy mother.

"No. Apparently, in a short time, The Hammer Family acquired some pretty rabid fans. And apparently, I ticked one of them off pretty bad. The day after I signed with Sequin, I got the first letter. I wasn't living here yet, and it came to my old address. The second one came to this address, and I don't know how he got it. I'm assuming it's a he—"

"You have the letters?" he interrupted.

She shuffled some papers around on her coffee table and produced one wrinkled, lined piece of paper. "Only the newest one."

"How many have there been?"

"This is the third. The police kept the first two. But they so obviously didn't care that I didn't even tell them about the third one."

"You should," he said quickly. "There may be evidence on this one that aren't on the other two." He looked down at the well-handled piece of paper. If there had been any evidence on it, she had probably destroyed it by now.

In neat, unnecessarily large cursive, it read: You abandoned your family and fans. You don't deserve to live the life you're living.

Yikes. He looked up at her. "This came regular mail?"

She nodded.

"Can I see the envelope?"

She got up and went into her small kitchen area.

He looked around and appraised the open layout. It had looked bigger from the outside. Of course, it was difficult to judge size with all the condos smashed together. He liked the openness of the central living area and wondered how many other rooms there were. From where he sat, he found it hard to believe she'd have room to house him. Maybe she was going to put him in a closet. He didn't love small spaces. He told himself that a closet in this place would still be bigger than his barracks had been. That idea helped a little.

He looked out the giant window that offered no privacy. "Do those drapes shut?" he asked without looking at her.

"Yeah."

"You should shut them."

She didn't move, so he looked at her. She looked put out.

"You want me to shut them?"

She sighed and went to the corner of the room, where she pulled a cord. The room fell into near-darkness. The only light shown from a small bulb over her kitchen sink. "Happy?" she snipped.

He didn't like her tone, but he hid this. She might be a handful, but if she was going to pay him, it would be worth it. "Can't afford to turn on the other lights?"

Her head jerked back like she'd been slapped. Shoot. He'd been kidding. He hadn't meant to offend her. He'd assumed that, living in a place like this, she must be flush. A different scenario hadn't occurred to him. He wondered then how much this gig paid, but he didn't think this was the time to ask.

She turned on an overhead light and then handed him an envelope. He looked at it carefully, but it was nondescript. No return address, of course, a common stamp, postmarked Dallas. "Who do you know in Texas?"

She tipped her head to the side. "I'm *from* Texas. Everyone I know is in Texas."

She really should have given this to the police. "Tell me about the first letters."

She plopped down onto the sofa and looked at the ceiling. "Let's see. The first one said, 'How dare you? Go back to your family or you'll regret it.' And the second one said, 'Your fans will never forgive this. You should be ashamed.'"

"A man of few words."

"Yep. You two have something in common."

He looked up at her quickly, wondering if she was accusing him of something, but her eyes looked playful. He set the letter and envelope on the table and leaned back in his chair. Since he'd read the ad, he'd wanted this job for the money. Now he wanted it because he needed to protect her. This guy, whoever he was, shouldn't be able to get near this woman. "What else would you like to know about me?"

Her eyes scanned his paperwork. "I think your resume tells me enough. Skilled in martial arts ... you have a carry permit in several states, obviously know how to use a gun, though I hope you won't need to. You don't have much bodyguard experience, but eight years in the service over-qualifies you." She looked up at him. "Why did you leave the army?"

His stomach tightened. He did not want to answer this question. "It was time."

She didn't look satisfied. "Do you mind driving? I don't have a chauffeur. I don't have anyone, actually. Yet. It would be just you."

He preferred driving, actually. "You don't have a manager?"

"Oh yeah, of course. But he's rarely around. And you'll go on tour with me?"

He'd been worried about this, with her being a hot, new artist. Of course she would be going on tour. And it wasn't the tour itself he was worried about—he'd done plenty of tours. It was the nightmares. And the tight quarters of a tour bus. "When?"

"Next week. We'll be gone for at least two months, hopefully more."

He nodded, trying to keep his reservations hidden.

She looked confused. "So ... do you want the job?"

Well, *that* was easy. "Absolutely."

She cocked a cute eyebrow. "Don't you want to know what it pays?"

Of course he did.

She shuffled some more papers around and then handed him two documents, each stapled separately. The top one was a confidentiality agreement. The second was a contract. He scanned it, looking for the salary, which he found on page two. Yikes again. It was half of what Kate had paid him. He looked up at the young country music star. Was she a tightwad or was she struggling? Turned out it didn't matter to him. "Where do I sign?"

# 3

Maggie handed the hunk a pen and allowed herself to exhale. He was taking the job. Thank God. She was surprised he was willing to work for so little money. Maybe he was having trouble finding a job without Kate Leece's endorsement. She wished she knew Kate, so she could ask for the inside scoop, but she didn't, and most people in the business were now treating her like some sort of pariah. Didn't they understand that she hadn't done anything wrong? It didn't matter. She would prove herself to them all. And she would give Dane a raise as soon as she could.

Maggie wasn't even worried that he might be a bit of a loose cannon. She hoped he'd learned his lesson, but even if he hadn't—she'd rather have a hothead beside her than a complacent professional who'd been in the business too long. She didn't want to be scared of the letter writer—but she was.

Besides, truth be told, she was a bit of a hothead herself.

He signed the nondisclosure without reading it. That seemed reasonable; she hadn't read it either. She'd printed it off the Internet that morning. "Would you like to see your room?"

He nodded and stood up.

She led the way back toward the front door. "Now, when we're in Nashville, you don't need to stay here all the time. I know no one can work every hour of every day. Just let me know in advance, and I'll find a substitute for you, so you can have some time off." She had no idea how she would pay the substitute. She didn't even know how she was going to pay Dane.

She opened the door to his room. The real estate agent had told her it was supposed to be an office, but she had brought in a bed and a dresser and called it a bedroom. "Sorry, there's no closet." There were, however, plenty of outlets. "We can get you a television if you want one." Shoot. Why hadn't she thought of that before?

"Not much for TV." His face was impassive.

She couldn't tell if he was okay with the room or not. "You can move your stuff here too, as much as you want. You don't have to use this furniture if you don't want to. I'm not attached to it. I mean, I won't be offended if you don't want ..." She stopped. Why was she babbling? She feared his sparse speech was creating gaps of silence that her lips were rushing to fill.

"Don't have much. This is fine."

Oh good. She'd gotten him to say two sentences.

"Want me to start now?"

She nodded. "If that's all right with you."

"Can I get your schedule? As far out in advance as you have it. Times, addresses, and who you expect to be at each event."

She didn't know any of that stuff. She wasn't exactly organized. Her predisposition to disarray must have shown on her face.

"Just get me as much as you can. The more I can prepare, the better. Can I take a look at your vehicle?"

Grateful for a task she could handle, she eagerly led him to her parking spot and the brand-new Ruby Red Ford Expedition that occupied it.

He whistled. "Nice wheels."

Her cheeks got hot. They *were* nice wheels. And she'd only made one payment on them. Her second payment was two weeks late. The thought of repossession kept her up nights. Not because she'd miss the vehicle, which she would, but because she wasn't sure she'd survive the embarrassment.

"What?" he asked.

She looked up at him and squinted. He was standing directly in front of the sun, and she could barely see his face with the ring of blinding light around it. She put a hand over her eyes, but it didn't help much. "What, what?"

"What are you not telling me?"

So much. There was so much she was not telling him. She didn't know where to start.

"Never mind." He held out his hand with his palm up. "We can talk about it when I come inside."

Why was he holding out his hand? Did he want her to slap him five?

"Keys?"

Oh. Duh. She'd forgotten that. Her heart sank. She hated looking stupid. "Be right back." She turned to hurry inside, leaving her new bodyguard standing beneath his halo.

# 4

Dane stared at the giant red SUV in front of him as he waited for his new charge to fetch the keys. He wished she had a locked garage. Though even an unlocked garage would be better than this parking spot out in the wide open. He also wished her vehicle were a bit more nondescript. But this thing *would* be fun to drive. He could talk her into a gray model later. He smirked at the thought of her. She was proving to be a bit of a ditz. A beautiful ditz, but still a ditz. But what had he expected? Artists were artists. That's why they needed people like him. Besides, she was probably a little rattled from the letters. What kind of creep would write such things? His experiences so far had shown him that country music fans were usually reasonable people. He was one himself, and he was reasonable—usually.

He heard the clicking of her high heels and turned to see her holding a pink, sparkly, furry key chain out toward him. He would have to accidentally lose that thing soon. It wouldn't fit into his pocket. He grudgingly took it from her hand and clicked a button on the fob. He opened the door and started the vehicle, wondering why Maggie was still standing there watching him. Didn't she have better things to do? He looked in the glove compartment, under the dash, under the seats, in the center console—

"What are you looking for?" she called.

He didn't answer her. He didn't mean to be rude, but he wasn't much for talking just to talk, and he didn't know what he was looking for. He was just looking. He opened the rear hatch and checked the seat folding compartments. There was nothing there. He hadn't expected there to be, but if he hadn't checked, there would have been something there.

When he stood up straight, Maggie was gone. This was mostly a relief. He didn't like being stared at. He finished his inspection in peace, checking under the hood and then under the actual truck, but he didn't find anything out of place. The vehicle seemed to have just rolled off the assembly line.

With the Ford deemed safe, he locked it back up and headed inside, where he found Maggie sitting on the couch listening to music. She had her laptop in her lap. She stared down at it, her brow furrowed in concentration. Her legs stretched out in front of her, and her feet rested on her coffee table, with her perfectly pedicured pink toenails pointing toward the ceiling. Her body's position suggested she was comfortable, but her body was rigid, her jaw tight.

"Catchy," he said.

She jumped and looked up at him.

"Sorry," he said quickly. "Didn't mean to startle you." Was she always this oblivious to her surroundings? He hadn't exactly sneaked up on her.

"You think it's catchy? I'm not so impressed. But I've still got to pick two more tracks for my album, which was supposed to come out, like, *yesterday*. So maybe this is the one. I could certainly do it better than this chick."

He nodded, feeling a moment of sympathy for the anonymous demo singer. "Your new label in a hurry?"

"In a hurry to make the millions off me that they're going to make? Yeah, of course. But I'm in a hurry too. I'm in my prime. It's a waste of time to wait."

So she wasn't much for humility. He didn't really mind her confidence, though. She was beautiful and talented—why not be a little cocky? That was better than false humility. "Mind if I look around?"

She waved both hands out to her sides, making the gesture look like a dance move.

It occurred to him that Maggie Hammer found all of life to be a stage. Wasn't that a line from a poem he'd been forced to read in high school? Shakespeare maybe?

"Be my guest," she said with a flirtatious smile.

Was it getting really warm in there? "I need to check the bedroom too. Is that okay?"

"*Mi casa es tu casa*," she said, mispronouncing every syllable.

He tried to hide his smile as he went into the bedroom first. Might as well get it over with. He was surprised to note that the room was skimpily appointed: mattress on the floor with a single sheet and blanket, and some clothes and shoes scattered around the carpet, but no dresser or vanity or entertainment system. The closet stood open, and a few outfits hung from hangers, but not nearly as many as one would expect to see in a diva's closet.

*She may be successful, but she's not wealthy.* This realization made him feel better about his new salary. It also made him wonder where her money was going. Booze? Drugs? Gambling? Any of those things would make his job much harder. He was willing to sacrifice his life for someone else's, but not in the name of a drug deal. He returned to the living room and sat down across from his new boss. "Let's talk about money."

# 5

Maggie's stomach plummeted. He hadn't even worked for her for an hour yet, and he was going to quit. She wondered why the delayed reaction to learning his salary, but she didn't have the energy to analyze him. "What?" she snapped.

He recoiled just a bit and held up both his hands as if to fend off her attack. "I'm not trying to pry. I just need to know all the facts if I'm going to do my job."

What? This didn't sound like salary talk. "What do you mean?"

"I spent enough time with Kate to get an idea of how country stars live. This isn't it."

How dare he? What a jerk! "I just moved in here. Judge much?"

The corners of his eyes drooped, making him look sad all of a sudden. She didn't like that look, which was odd. She rarely cared when other people were sad. Unless they were children. She couldn't stand sad children.

"I'm not judging you, Maggie. I would never do that. But you've only got two pairs of shoes in there. So you've either got a secret stash of shoes, or you're broke."

She jumped to her feet and put her hands on her hips. "I don't need to take this from you!" she spat. She was so angry, her brain couldn't come up with anything more original to say.

He leaned back in his chair, and his expression softened. "And I don't need to take this from you. Either sit down and we'll have an adult conversation or I will leave just as easily as I came in."

"Are you calling me a child?" She really wished her voice would stop squeaking. It was hard to insist she wasn't a child when she sounded like one. She stood over him glaring down at him, wondering what her next move should be. She wasn't even sure why she was so offended. Because he had called her out? Because he was right? Because how dare he have the gall to question her when she was the boss? She was new to this whole being a boss thing. It wasn't as much fun as she'd thought it would be.

He stared at her, unflinching. Were they having a staring contest? If so, she thought she might lose. Something about staring into his eyes made her feel weak. Weakness was a feeling she could not tolerate.

Because she didn't know what else to do, she sat back down.

"I don't care about how successful you are or how much money you make. My only mission is to protect you. And I can't protect you if I don't know what shady dealings you're involved with."

A cackle erupted out of her. "Shady dealings? Are you out of your mind?"

He furrowed his brow. "The money has to go somewhere. In my experience, that usually means self-medicating." His voice was full of emotion. Either he self-medicated or he knew someone who did.

"I don't self-medicate."

"Then," he said, his words slow and even, "where does the money go?"

She leaned forward and glared at him, and said, imitating his speech pattern with slow and deliberate words. "There. Is. No. Money."

His eyes widened as he leaned back in his chair.

Good. She'd rendered him speechless. Trouble was, she couldn't think of anything to say either.

After a long silence that wasn't as uncomfortable as she expected, he said, "How is that possible?"

Her eyes filled with tears, and she hated herself for them. "It's not that simple. Newcomers in this business need to make sacrifices to get where they want to be. I'm going all the way to the top. How much I make today doesn't really matter because I'll be making plenty then."

"But you're *not* a newcomer. Didn't you get paid for those Hammer Family hits?"

"Not really."

His face registered surprise. Of course. Here it was again—the blind belief in the snow-white Hammer Family image. She was so sick of that image she could cry. Or puke. Or both.

"Is that why you left?"

"I left for a million reasons. I never wanted to be there in the first place."

"Maggie, if your mother kept your money, you have legal recourse."

She didn't know if that was true. "I don't care about the money." She really didn't. But even if she did, she didn't want to involve herself with more family drama. She didn't even want to be associated with The Hammer Family. She would've changed her name, but her new label wouldn't let her. Maggie Hammer? What kind of a name was that? Rock stars weren't named Maggie Hammer. Catholic school teachers were named Maggie Hammer.

"That's admirable. You didn't get any money for signing with the new label?"

She shook her head slowly. "Not yet." And she knew it would be a while before she would get any money from them. She hadn't gotten a good deal with her contract. Her manager had advised her to not sign, to wait for something better, but she didn't have time to wait. The days of her life, the *years* of her life, were ticking by her. The older she got, the harder it would be to make the climb.

# 6

Dane didn't understand. Country music was a lucrative business. How could this woman be broke? His curiosity was certainly piqued, but he also knew that this was none of his business. "So, no drugs?"

"Of course not," she said quickly.

"And no drinking?"

She tilted her head to the side and gave him a sardonic look. "I'm not a prude."

He chuckled, despite himself. He couldn't stand the stuff himself, but he didn't mind if she drank a bit, as long as it wasn't problematic. "Well, your tour will start soon, and that should bring in some money. Who are we going out with?"

She cocked one perfectly groomed eyebrow. "Going out with? No one. I don't open."

He didn't think she was a big enough deal yet to headline, but he didn't want to say that. So he said nothing.

She read his mind. "I'm not playing stadiums or anything. I will be, though. Soon."

Aha. Visions of him trying to pull her through crowds of drunks at local dives flashed through his mind. "So, where are we playing?"

"Theaters, clubs. Don't worry—nowhere sketchy."

He nodded. "And are you bringing an opening act?" He felt sorry for whoever it was.

"Blayze Balin."

*Talk about sketchy.* "You're kidding."

She tipped her head back and chuckled. Her hair fell in loose curls behind her head and quivered as she laughed. The sight of it made his chest warm, a feeling he didn't appreciate.

"Hey, I know he's a jerk, but the women love him. Besides, think of the media coverage our combination could get."

He could imagine it, but he wasn't sure it would be positive attention. This reminded him of something. "Hey, weren't you seeing Cole Washburne?"

She rolled her eyes. "That guy is an idiot. I only wanted to hook up with him because I knew I was going solo and wanted him for my brand. But he turned out to be a bit too boring, and he chose some crazy waitress over me. So don't even say his name again." She stared into the corner of the room. Then, as an afterthought, she added, "We're still friends, though."

He snickered. He had no idea what that meant and thought probably Cole Washburne didn't even know he was still friends with Maggie Hammer. "You date people for your brand?"

"Why else would I date them?" She seemed to realize how awful that sounded. "It's not really dating. Everything is about my brand. All that matters is my career. I don't have time or energy for relationships. Besides"—she made a *pfft* sound as she blew her bangs away from her face—"men are stupid."

He chose not to be offended by that. "So you're going to try to date Blayze? Just for the attention?" The idea made him sick to his stomach.

She winked at him. "I guess we'll have to see what happens."

"Doesn't that guy get kicked off tours all the time? For partying and destroying hotel rooms?"

"Like I said, we'll see what happens." She appeared to be excited by the idea of revelry and destruction. He realized then that this job wouldn't be easy. Yet, he still needed it. At least he wouldn't be bored.

"Can I have the tour schedule?"

"I already emailed it to you."

"And the rest of your schedule?"

She looked at him as if he were stupid. "You just asked me for that like two seconds ago. I said I'll get it to you and I'll get it to you."

He ignored her snippiness and remained professional. "Do you own the tour bus? Or are we renting?"

"Don't know the details. The label has some tour manager doing all that."

"I need to inspect the bus when I can. Is the label sending security?"

She shook her head slowly.

"Do they know about this threat?"

She shook her head again.

"Why not?"

She took a deep breath. "I didn't want to give them any reason not to sign me. And I don't want to give them any reason to drop me."

He didn't think they'd drop her over an issue many celebrities had. "Drop you? Don't you have a contract?"

"Contracts can be broken. They bought me out of the one I had with Evelyn Records."

Dane whistled. "That must have cost a pretty penny."

She shrugged. "I'm worth it."

There was that humility again. "Okay, what do you need from me today?"

"I need you to keep me from getting kidnapped or killed while I finish listening to these terrible songs."

Okay then. She seemed to flip-flop between sweet and snarky. He stood to leave the room. "Let me know if you need anything."

"I have to be at the studio by one o'clock tonight."

"One?" Why that late?

"Those are the cheapest studio hours. And the only ones we could get before I leave. So, let me pick the song I'm going to record tonight. Please." It was the most disingenuous please he'd ever heard.

He left the room without another word and went outside to check the perimeter of her building. He also needed to go talk to the security personnel standing at the edge of her drive, guarding this small gated community that he now knew she couldn't even afford to live in.

# 7

Maggie listened to every single demo song and hated every single demo song. She couldn't believe this was the best her people could come up with. Were they scraping the bottom of the barrel with her? Giving her songs everyone else had already passed on? Didn't they understand she was trying to build a specific brand here? She wanted to be the superstar men wanted and women wanted to be. With these songs, men wouldn't even notice her and women would roll their eyes at her. She dragged the last one into the trash can, finding the little crumpling sound her laptop made incredibly satisfying.

She needed two songs.

She had none.

She was supposed to record one tonight.

She didn't have one.

She needed to write her own song.

She had no idea how to do such a thing.

She found a notebook and pencil and returned to the couch. She picked up her mandolin and then changed her mind and picked up the guitar. No one wrote songs with a mandolin, right? She strummed a few chords and tried to think of something to say. What did she want to say to the world? What was going on in her heart rate now? Ambition. She had goals. She wanted to climb that mountain. Oh shoot. Hadn't Reba already cut a mountain climbing song? What metaphor could she use other than mountain? She had to cross that river. No. That wouldn't work. Cross the desert? No, that was even dumber. Okay, forget the goals metaphor. What could represent ambition? Immediately, one of her favorite songs entered her brain:

"I'm Gonna Be Somebody." Obviously, that had been done too. Was there anything that hadn't been done? How did songwriters do this?

She shook her head. Time to start over. Forget writing about what was in her heart. She just needed a fresh idea. She closed her eyes and thought. What was fresh? Vegetables. Vegetables were fresh. But she couldn't write a song about vegetables, unless she was changing her target demographic to preschoolers.

What did other songwriters write about? Love. She grunted. That wasn't going to happen. She didn't even believe in love. They wrote about heartbreak. She knew plenty about that, but she didn't want to go there. It wasn't on-brand. Cheating. Could she write a cheating song? She had never been in a relationship long enough to get cheated on, and if she was ever foolish enough to get caught up in a relationship, she knew she wouldn't cheat on someone. Besides, that wasn't really on-brand either. Good grief, this was hard. What else did people write about? Dirt roads, beer, Jesus—nope, her family had done enough Jesus songs to last her a lifetime—dogs, trains, prison, death, grief, abuse ... She threw the guitar to the end of the couch and opened her laptop again. She dragged "The Keys to My Heart" out of her trashcan and brought it back to life. It was a terrible song. It would have to do. Songwriting was for the birds.

She got herself a glass of tap water, which tasted terrible. The only thing she missed about her Texas home was the well water. It was sweet. Someone should write a song about that someday. She sat back down and concentrated on learning the song, singing it over and over until she was so sick of it she wanted to cry. She wondered where Dane was and if her singing was annoying him. She hoped he didn't mind her voice; he would be hearing a lot of it.

It was getting late. She should probably try to get some sleep. She lay down on the couch and pulled a throw blanket over her face.

Her brain was racing. She tried to calm it down, tried to think about nothing, tried to relax and fall asleep, but it wasn't happening.

She was worried about the stupid keys song. It would probably just be an album cut, but it still wasn't good enough. Not being able to even start writing a song made her feel like a country music impostor. She was a better musician and a better singer than almost everyone else in the business, but her inability to create something from scratch felt like a black gaping hole in her potential. Even Blayze was a songwriter. Maybe they could spend some time together on the road and write together. Maybe with his help, she could actually create something—or contribute to something that he created. Or maybe she could charm him into thinking she was helping, and just ride his coattails to getting her name on a song. She was thrilled to be going out on tour with Blayze, but she was also concerned. He was always in trouble. She thought this would keep her name in the country news, but she hoped it didn't backfire. Thinking about Blayze made her think about Dane: good grief, he was handsome. She squeezed her eyes shut tighter. No need to be thinking like that. She wondered how Dane and Blayze would get along, and then wondered why that mattered. It didn't. She wondered what Dane would think of her new song, but then realized that didn't matter either, and then she was back to worrying about how bad the new song really was.

She sat up. Lying down was useless. Her brain wouldn't slow down, let alone shut off.

She looked at the clock. It was too early to go to the studio, but she thought she'd go anyway. Maybe she could sit in on the session before her. Or at least they could go get coffee. She went to knock on Dane's door.

As she approached his room, she heard him talking. She assumed he was on the phone, but then she realized he wasn't making any sense. She strained to make out his words, but it sounded like he was telling someone to get down, and he kept saying no, no, no. It wasn't loud, but he certainly sounded distressed. Concerned, she knocked on his door loudly. At first, there was no response.

Then the door was yanked open and she was looking up at a disheveled but wide-eyed Dane.

"Are you okay?" she asked.

"Of course. What do you need?"

"I was hoping we could head out early. I can't sleep." She felt guilty then, an emotion she rarely experienced. Just because she couldn't sleep didn't mean that Dane couldn't. But it was too late now. "Sorry to wake you."

"Give me sixty seconds." He turned away from her and picked up his boots.

She smiled. Why had he said sixty seconds? Why not a minute? He was a little adorable—*oh my gosh, I need to stop thinking about how handsome and adorable he is. He is just the hired help.* She really needed to get some sleep. "Actually, I'm not even ready yet. I just thought I'd give you warning that I wanted to leave early." She still had to fix her hair and makeup.

He looked her up and down. "You look great."

Her cheeks got hot, and she didn't know why. People complimented her looks all the time. "Thanks," she said softly, "but I'll just be a minute."

He put on his coat and stepped out of his room. "Let me go outside and look around. I'll come back for you."

She thought he was probably being overprotective. But she had never felt safer in her life.

# 8

Dane hadn't meant to fall asleep. He'd been lying there listening to Maggie sing, and he'd just nodded off. This was a good thing, as he rarely slept, but a bad thing because, of course, it had led to his nightmares. He wondered if he'd called out in his sleep again. He thought he probably had, as she'd looked concerned and asked him if he was okay. He was embarrassed, but there wasn't much he could do about it, except sleep as little as possible. His stomach rolled at the thought of the tight quarters of the tour bus. Never mind sleeping as little as possible—he'd have to try not to sleep at all. For the most part, this wouldn't be a problem. He'd worked lots of days on no sleep. Still, he hoped they would get an occasional hotel room so he'd be able to catch up. A few times, when he'd been deployed, he'd gone for so long without sleep that he'd started to hallucinate. He'd once seen a dragon in the desert. That wouldn't be a good thing in his current circumstances. He didn't need to be seeing dragons in Maggie Hammer's mosh pit.

"What?" she asked, yanking him out of his head.

He looked over at her. The dim lights from the dashboard gave her an ethereal glow, made her look *softer*. She really was beautiful, and probably would be, even without all the paint and glitter. He pulled his eyes back to the road without answering her.

"You were smiling."

"Oh."

"Why were you smiling?"

He couldn't tell her he was smiling about dragons in her mosh pit, so he said nothing.

"You really need to talk more."

He had nothing to say to that either.

"Fine," she snapped.

Oops. He hadn't meant to offend her. "Sorry."

It was her turn to be quiet.

Upon her request, he took her through a coffee house drive through. She leaned across his lap to speak out the window, and her hair smelled like strawberries. He tried not to notice. She ordered a Cinnamon Dolce Latte with an extra shot of espresso. He thought about telling her that she'd be able to pay him better if she spent less on coffee. Of course, he didn't.

"Do you want anything?" she asked, still leaning over him, looking at him now, her face only inches from his own.

He wondered what it would be like to kiss her, and this thought horrified him. Why had he thought that? "No," he said with too much emphasis.

Her head recoiled, but came right back. "Are you sure? My treat."

He was still thinking about her lips, no matter how hard he tried not to. "No," he said again.

She finally gave up. "That's all," she said out the window, and then quickly slid back to her own seat. "You're kind of rude."

*You're one to talk.* "Thank you for the offer, but I don't do caffeine." He pulled the SUV ahead to the window.

"Are you serious? I thought soldiers mainlined the stuff."

"Some do." He couldn't tell her more. Couldn't tell his new boss that caffeine made his PTSD worse, that it made him jumpier, that he already had enough anxiety to deal with without feeding his worn out adrenal glands anxiety juice.

She handed him her debit card, and he passed it to the woman in the window, who snatched it out of his hand. The coffee smelled good drifting out through the open window, making him wonder, not for the first time, why coffee smelled so much better than it tasted. Few other foods or beverages could make that claim. Dark chocolate, maybe.

"Why don't you drink coffee?"

*This woman is uncomfortable with silence.* "It's not good for you."

"Are you a health nut?"

*Hardly.* He loved Ben & Jerry's far too much for that. "No."

The woman handed him a tall paper cup that wasn't nearly tall enough to justify its price tag, and he thanked her as he handed it across the large vehicle to his new boss. Now the truck smelled like strawberry coffee. He wondered if anyone made such a thing. He knew they made blueberry and cherry—why not strawberry? Maybe he could invent the stuff and not need to risk his life for a living anymore.

He eased the truck back out into traffic, and Maggie gave him directions to the studio.

"You know that we're early, right?"

"Of course I know that. I can tell time. But I'm sure someone is in there recording, and I'm hoping they'll let me observe."

"They let people do that?"

"Sure. I don't know if they'll let *me* do that, but I'm going to give it a shot."

"Why?"

"Why what?"

"Why do you want to watch someone else sing into a microphone?"

"Because I can learn from watching others," she said, as if that had been as stupid question.

Her answer shocked him. He figured that, in her estimation, she already knew all there was to know.

"What?" she asked, sounding paranoid.

"I didn't say anything."

"I know. But you were thinking it. I could feel you. You were thinking judgy thoughts."

He chuckled. "No, I wasn't."

"Then what were you thinking?"

He took a deep breath. Would there always be constant chatter with this woman? Or would she get used to him and start to let him blend into the background like Kate had done? "I was just surprised to hear you say you wanted to learn. Pleasantly surprised. You don't seem lacking in the confidence department."

"I'm not," she snapped, almost before he'd finished his sentence. "I'm confident, but I'm not stupid. I know I have lots to learn about this business ... *and* about being an artist. And I am hungry to learn it. I know that I have the talent, more than most people have, but plenty of talented people don't live up to their potential. So I'm going to be a good student and work my butt off so I live up to mine."

*Well put*, he thought, as he pulled the truck into the parking lot of the studio.

His stomach fell. He recognized the Mercedes-Benz parked in front of the door. If it didn't belong to Kate Leece, it sure did look a lot like hers. He said a silent prayer that it was someone else's red convertible as he turned off the engine. "Let me get out and look around. Then I'll open the door for you." The parking lot was large and well lit, and he didn't anticipate any trouble, but still, he wanted to be careful.

She didn't say anything.

He didn't think that being thorough would irritate her under the circumstances. He didn't sense anything or anyone out of place in the parking lot, so he opened the SUV's door for her, and she stepped out onto the pavement, one long leg at a time. He caught himself watching those legs and willed himself to look at the stars, which he couldn't see very many of, thanks to the same parking lot lights that afforded the extra sense of safety he appreciated. "After you," he said, and motioned to the door.

He followed her to the entrance and stood back while she pressed the buzzer and announced herself. To his surprise, the door clicked open.

But when they got to the lobby, a young, frazzled-looking woman said, "You are more than an hour early." The nameplate on the welcome counter read, "Dottie—Reception."

"I know," Maggie said with a brightness he knew was fake. "I was hoping I could sit in and listen on the current session."

Dottie scowled, confirming Dane's suspicion that this was not a common practice. "I'll ask." She vanished down a hallway, and it was obvious that she expected Maggie and Dane to wait in the lobby, but Maggie wasn't much of a waiter. She just followed the receptionist, so Dane followed them both.

Dottie stopped at a door and gave a perfunctory knock before opening it three inches. As she delivered Maggie's request to whoever was inside, a door farther down the hallway opened, and Kate Leece stepped out. Dane's stomach sank, mostly from embarrassment. He'd never been fired from anything before, and he was mortified that he'd been fired by her.

Kate started when she saw him, then looked at Maggie and grimaced. "Well, well, well. Isn't this a match made in heaven?"

Maggie rushed forward, her hand extended. "Kate! It's so nice to meet you. I'm a big fan."

Kate graciously shook her hand, but said, "I appreciate that, but I can't say the same."

Dane knew Kate, and she didn't usually speak to people like that. What was wrong with her?

"Excuse me?" Maggie said, with over-the-top indignation.

"I'm a fan of your *mother's*," Kate said, "and I'm a fan of your family's. So I wasn't impressed with your little tantrum."

Maggie stepped closer to her and lowered her chin. "You don't know anything about my mother," she almost hissed.

Dane couldn't believe it, but it appeared that an altercation was brewing, and he stepped forward in case he had to intervene. He was feeling incredibly protective of Maggie all of a sudden. And yes, that was his job. But his job was *physical* protection. Not social protection, or emotional protection, or even professional protection. And he knew Kate posed no physical threat to Maggie. So why were his hackles raised?

Dottie reappeared behind them. "I'm sorry, Miss Hammer, you'll have to come back at your scheduled time."

Kate gave Dottie an amused glance over Maggie's shoulder and then turned her eyes to Dane. "So this is where you ended up, huh? No one else would take her?"

Not exactly. More like no one else would take Maggie's paycheck. But Dane stayed silent. Silence was always safer.

Kate looked at Maggie. "You know what?" she said, abruptly changing her tone. "Why don't you step into the live room with me for a second?" She turned back toward the door she'd come out through and then looked at Dane. "I'll have her back to you in a jiffy."

# 9

*What is going on?* Maggie wondered, almost panicking. The woman obviously hated her, and now she wanted to have a private chat in a sound-proof room? This could only go one way, and Maggie didn't want to get caught in the current. Still, she couldn't say no to *Kate Leece!* The woman was an industry veteran, a talented showman with great connections. So, Maggie followed her into the room and heard the door click shut behind them. Maggie looked to her right, at the two men in the control room.

Kate put a hand on her hip and leveled a gaze at Maggie. "Don't worry about them. They aren't listening."

They didn't appear to be, but how could Maggie be sure?

"Look. I know you're young, and that's probably why you left your mother in the lurch."

Maggie opened her mouth to protest, but Kate didn't give her a chance.

"But women in this business need to watch out for each other, so I'm going to do you a favor and tell you to fire your new muscle."

Maggie's chest tightened, and she rolled her shoulders back. "Dane told me all about what happened with you, and I'm sorry that happened, but it was a mistake, and I'm not going to hold it against—"

"Dane told you about *one* thing that happened?" Kate interrupted. "Oh, honey, there was more than *one* thing. The man is unstable, and he may do a great job of keeping you safe, but you might not be safe from *him*."

Maggie had no idea how to respond to that. She had known Dane for a matter of hours, yet she was one hundred percent certain he posed no threat to her. "Why would you say such a thing?"

Kate furrowed her brow. "Because it's the truth."

"I know the guy caused you some trouble, but he's still a person. He's still a professional, and you're trying to ruin his career."

Kate tipped her head back and cackled at the high ceiling. Then she returned her scalding eyes to Maggie's. "He has no career. At least not in Nashville. He can go work security at a roller rink. I'm not ruining anything. I'm trying to help you."

Maggie didn't know whether this was true. Did Kate actually believe what she was saying?

"And you'd be more likely to listen to me if you weren't all gaga for the guy."

*What?* Maggie's mouth fell open. "I am not *gaga* for the guy." And she wasn't. Why had Kate said that?

"Oh sure, his looks had *nothing* to do with you picking him out of the resume pile."

Maggie laughed sardonically. Kate had no idea just how small that resume pile had been. "Whatever." She wanted to walk away, but her curiosity wouldn't let her. "What did he do?"

Kate dramatically folded her arms across her chest. "You don't want me to soil the man's reputation, but you want me to give you specifics?"

Maggie rolled her eyes. All of a sudden, she could not *stand* Kate Leece, no matter how many CMA trophies she had on her shelf. "Yes. If you want me to fire someone, then I want specifics."

"Sugar, I don't care if you fire him or not. I was just trying to help. The specifics are that he is mentally ill. He's so scared of his own nightmares that he doesn't sleep, and then he's jumpy and unpredictable during the day. You don't want to be the one he's looking at when he decides there's an imaginary threat."

Maggie thought her heart might explode. How dare this woman speak about any veteran like that? She opened her mouth to tell her where to stick it, but Kate cut her off.

"Get out of my studio. I have work to do." She spun away from Maggie and put on her headphones.

Maggie stood rooted to her spot, feeling spurned and helpless.

Kate spoke into the microphone, "I'm ready."

One of the men on the other side of the window turned to face her then, granting Maggie a little relief that maybe Kate had been right. Maybe they hadn't been listening. For Dane's sake, Maggie hoped not. She forced her feet to carry her back out into the hallway, where Dane stood at attention, a concerned look on his face.

"We need to talk," she said, and headed for the door.

She stepped out into the cool night air and walked toward a stone bench on the lawn, without checking to see if Dane was following. She knew that he was.

At first, he just stood beside the bench, but then she patted the seat beside her. "Have a seat."

"It's not safe here." He didn't sit.

"Yes, it is." She had no idea. "Sit down."

He sat, but he looked incredibly uncomfortable. His eyes darted around from tree to tree.

She wondered if he was seeing things that weren't there, but then silently scolded herself for thinking that. That wasn't fair to him. "So, Kate's not a fan."

He didn't say anything.

She really wished he'd talk more. "You were a soldier." She paused.

After several seconds, he said, "Was that a question?"

"Not really." She'd already known that of course. It had been on his resume. Why had she asked that? She scanned her brain for the right words. "Look, I'm sorry if this is rude, but I'm just going to come out with it."

He laughed.

"What's so funny?"

He looked at her, and returning his gaze felt like swimming in a warm pool. "You, worried about sounding rude." He looked back to the trees, and she missed his eyes.

"I don't *try* to be rude, Dane. It's just that some circumstances make it impossible not to be. Anyway, do you have PTSD?"

"Yes," he said quickly, his voice even.

His matter-of-fact response surprised her, and she didn't know what to say next. "What are your symptoms?"

He took a big breath. "Nothing that will interfere with my ability to do this job."

"I heard you talking in your sleep. Do you have nightmares?"

He nodded.

"And anxiety?"

He looked at her and gave her such a slight nod that she wondered if she'd imagined it.

"Do you see things that aren't there?"

He shook his head, again barely moving. "Only when I'm asleep."

She let out a long breath. This was good news. His symptoms weren't so different from her own, and she was already living with those. "Anything else?"

"No."

She knew he wanted the matter to be closed, but she wasn't ready. "Do you take medication?"

His jaw flexed. She'd annoyed him. "No."

"Do you talk to anyone?"

He looked at her. "Do I look like someone who would want to talk to someone?"

She giggled, without even really knowing why she'd giggled. It hadn't been funny, but it had been kind of cute, and even in this serious moment, being near Dane brought her a weird joy. "No, but I meant a professional. Do you have a therapist or a counselor?"

His jaw moved again. Was he grinding his teeth? "Everyone I came back with has PTSD. I'm not even in bad shape in comparison. I don't need to *talk* to anyone." He said the word "talk" as if it tasted bad in his mouth. "Besides, I've tried. And it didn't help. And I've tried several medications. They didn't help. I'm fine. If you want to fire me, fire me, but I'm telling you, I can do this job."

"I'm not going to fire you, Dane," she said softly. "Kate told me you were dangerous." Oops. Why had she said that? "I didn't believe her," she hurried to add. "But what she said made me worried about you. Not worried about your job performance, but about *you*. I wanted to make sure you were okay. I know a little about PTSD myself."

His head snapped toward her, a question in his eyes.

Now was not the time to answer that question, though. She would probably never answer that question, especially if he never asked it out loud.

# 10

Dane's ears were wide open. Did she just say she suffered from PTSD? Or did she mean that she knew someone who did? Maybe some member of her family she was in such an all-fired hurry to get away from? He waited for her to say more, but she didn't. For once, she was silent. He couldn't blame her. He didn't exactly love talking about his fears either. His chest fluttered with a sudden desire to rescue her from the direction of their conversation.

"Since we're having this heart to heart, why don't you tell me why you're so mad at your mother?"

She looked at him, her shiny eyes wide in the dim light. She obviously hadn't been expecting *that* question. She put her hands in her coat pocket and stretched her legs out in front of her. Then she studied her shoes. "I love my mother. More than most people would understand or believe." She paused. "*That's* why I'm so mad at her."

He snickered. "You know that doesn't make sense, right?"

She sucked in a lungful. "It makes perfect sense." Dramatic exhale. "But it's a long story."

He looked at the locked door behind them. "I think we've got time."

She smiled, and it was cute. She should smile more often. "I know everybody thinks we were this perfect little church family, but that isn't even close to true."

He waited for her to continue, surprised at how much he wanted her to.

Finally, she said, "It's my father. He's not a good man."

Dane's stomach clenched. He didn't like the sound of that.

"And my mom is a fool for staying with him. God handed her this big giant perfect escape route, with fame and money, and what does she do? She brings him along." Her voice cracked. "She is so stupid. I love her, but I can't stand how stupid she is. And then she's holding his hand and waving for the cameras like they're this good old-fashioned country couple, and it just made me want to vomit. I couldn't be a part of that lie for one more second."

He couldn't believe what he was hearing. *That* was why she'd left the family band? That surely wasn't the way the media had portrayed it.

She seemed to sense his doubt. "Okay, well, of *course* there was more to it than that."

He snickered. He leaned back on the bench, feeling something close to relaxation, but when he felt it, the shock of it jerked him back upright.

"Of course I also wanted to be able to control my own career. *I* was the one who wanted to be a country star. *I* was the one who loved country music, who spent my whole childhood pretending I was Martina McBride." She launched into the chorus of "Independence Day," and, sure enough, she did sound a little like the country great.

"You wanted to be a star but you never went to Nashville on your own?"

"I couldn't," she snapped. "I couldn't leave my mother with him."

Dane considered his words even more carefully than usual. "Did he hit her?"

"Did he?" she repeated. "He did. And he does. Though I suppose all the cameras are slowing him down."

Dane ground his jaw. He hoped he didn't bump into this guy in the near future. Or ever. "Did he hit *you*?"

She looked at the ground, her lips clamped shut.

"And the boys?"

Still silent.

"Someone should turn him in. He'd do time. They'd be safe."

"No one will talk. They all want to protect him. It's ridiculous. Mom's been telling us our whole lives that he will get better, that he's struggling with a dark spirit, that we need to be loyal to him, not give up on him—I could go public, but no one would back my story up, and my mom would never speak to me again. And I don't think I could live with that." Her voice cracked again.

"She must be pretty mad about you leaving the group?"

Maggie shrugged. "Don't care so much about that. If she'd let me have *any* creative control, I might not have left."

He wanted her to say more.

She must have sensed it. "Mom was all about playing songs with strong instrumentals and blah lyrics. We cut an entire album and never said anything. At least, not anything that hasn't been said before. We're living with all this love and pain, and she refused to sing about it. I mean, I guess that's why Evelyn signed us, because they wanted that kind of stuff, but *I* don't want that kind of stuff. I want to say challenging things that make people think." She paused to catch her breath.

He found a new feeling forming in his chest. He was starting to respect her.

"You want to say something bold and honest?"

She nodded with vigor.

"Yet you're going to go in there in a few minutes and cut a song you hate?"

She was silent for a few seconds. "That's an excellent point."

Dane thought carefully. "You had fans when you were part of The Hammer Family. Now they're mad at you. And I'm not talking about that one crazy fan. I mean your real fans. They loved you a few months ago, when you were singing a certain type of song. Maybe you put a song like that on your new album, like a bridge to your new sound."

She studied his face as she processed his words. "That's not terribly crazy."

He smiled. "Thank you." It made him feel oddly good to offer musical advice. He'd loved music all his life, but he'd certainly never given advice to an actual artist. And it seemed she was even listening to it.

She folded her arms across her chest. "But what song? How am I going to find a strong instrumental song with blah lyrics in the next ten minutes?" She laughed. Then in a flash, she bounded off the bench and whirled to face him. "A cover song!"

He didn't know why she was quite *that* excited, but it did sound like a good idea.

"I know just the song. And it doesn't even have blah lyrics." She was bouncing up and down. She pulled her phone out of her back pocket and dialed someone. "Hey, can you get me the rights to 'Long Hard Road' like, *right now*?" She paused, presumably, to let whoever was on the other end of the phone tell her no. "Yeah, by Rodney Crowell." She paused again. "I know he'll let you," she argued. "He'll make a killing. Tell him everyone has forgotten that song but me, and I'll make him a zillion dollars with it."

Dane hoped the person on the other end would not use that *exact* language.

She hung up. "Let's make it happen!" She headed for the door, even though it wasn't yet time.

He hurried after her. "Will they let you record it before you get the rights?"

The door was still locked, and she turned to face him. "They won't know I don't have the rights!" She looked up at him, and her eyes were wild with excitement. He hadn't seen her like this before. "And I'll establish a relationship with Rodney, because there's another song of his I'd love to cut with Blayze—we could win vocal event of the year!"

He didn't know Rodney's music very well. "I don't think I know 'Long Hard Road.'"

"Nitty Gritty Dirt Band cut it." He blinked. She was talking really fast. "It was their first number one." Her expression turned grave. "I *love* Nitty Gritty."

He nodded, just barely keeping up with her. "I liked 'Fishin' in the Dark.'"

She grimaced. "Blah. That song was just fluff. 'Long Hard Road' has soul. And it depicts a loving family like the one everybody thinks I came from. It's perfect." She stood on her tiptoes and kissed him on the cheek.

Even as he knew this was wildly inappropriate, he immensely enjoyed it.

"Thanks, Dane. You're brilliant."

# 11

Maggie stepped up to the microphone with an excitement she hadn't felt before. Out of the ten songs she'd recorded so far, she truly loved only two of them. There were two more songs she thought could be big hits. The rest, she wasn't thrilled to admit, were just filler.

But she was *thrilled* to be tracking "Long Hard Road." She'd told her producer she'd already begun the process of acquiring rights, which was sort of true, and she'd shot Dane a warning look when he'd looked like he wanted to protest.

"What? I didn't say anything."

She must have heard him think it then.

And now here she was, with butterflies in her belly, about to cover one of the best bands in country music history. Probably *the* best. Yet another of her dreams coming true. She opened her mouth and sang the opening lyrics, allowing her own mind to drift back to her childhood, which caused her throat to close up a little, but she pushed through it, giving the lyrics more volume, and loved the gravelly sound of her voice as the pain shone through the beauty of the music. She closed her eyes and thought about growing up in small-town Texas, remembered staring out her bedroom window up at the moon. She couldn't wait to get out of that town. She couldn't wait to be someone, but even more importantly, to prove to everyone that she *could* be someone. Because they didn't treat her like that. They treated her like she was no one. She'd been invisible.

She knew she was going in too deep. She opened her eyes to bring herself back to the moment and found herself staring right at Dane, who stood leaning against the back of the sound room wall with his thick arms folded across his chest. He looked so serious. She flashed him a smile. She hadn't meant to. It had just happened, as if seeing him had made her smile. He smiled back, and butterflies soared through her chest.

What was going on? Why was her bodyguard giving her butterflies? That wasn't a good scenario. She convinced herself that she was just grateful to him for suggesting the song, and she tried to focus on bringing the outro home.

Indeed, she nailed it, and she stepped back from the mic feeling good about their first take.

"Good job," her producer said into her headset. "Ready for number two?"

She nodded, glancing at Dane without knowing why she was doing so.

"Great. Here we go."

She took a few deep breaths and then began to sing the song again, fervently hoping that the gravelly part of the first take made it into the final cut. She didn't allow herself to get as emotionally involved this time, and she wondered why her eyes kept drifting back toward Dane. This was probably only happening because he was staring at her.

"Do you need a break?" the producer interrupted her.

"No," she snapped, beyond annoyed. How dare he stop her in the middle of a song?

"You seem distracted. Do you need a rest? Or a drink of water?"

"I'm not distracted, I just started, so no, I don't need a rest, and no I don't need any water. What I *need* is to sing my song without interruption."

She heard the producer take his finger off his microphone button. He nodded at her, but it was obvious he was offended. She didn't care. He was getting paid by the hour, so he really shouldn't be dragging things out.

He pressed his button again. "Okay then, from the top."

She would never admit it, but she *had* been distracted. By Dane, of all things. So she vowed not to look at him as she sang this time. This proved more difficult than she'd thought it would be, so she turned her body to the side so that she wouldn't be so tempted. And then she tried to focus on the lyrics again—focus enough to sound good, but not enough to get all choked up again.

After five cuts, her producer asked her again if she needed a break, and again, she told him that she didn't.

After ten cuts, he told her to take a break while he talked to the engineer. Out of the corner of her eye, she saw Dane move and almost panicked, wondering where he was going and why he was leaving her. Then there was a knock on the door of the live room.

"Come in!"

Dane gingerly opened the door and then headed her way, holding a water bottle out in front of him. "How can you *not* need a drink after all that?"

She was thrilled at the sight, though she wasn't sure which sight was more welcome: the water, or the delivery man.

# 12

D ane slept better that night than he had in weeks. Though it had really been *morning* that he'd slept through. They'd gotten back from the studio at six, and he'd lain down for a rest and promptly fallen asleep. As far as he knew, his sleep had been dreamless. Maybe the little stone bench heart-to-heart with Maggie had been good for him, no matter how uncomfortable it had felt at the time.

He ducked across the hallway for a shower, and the house seemed cool and still. Maggie must still be sleeping. Good for her. She hadn't seemed especially tired when they'd gotten home, and he couldn't imagine how. Her first trip through the song had sounded perfect to him, and she was right—it *was* a great song. He hadn't heard the original, but he thought this might be one of those rare cases where the cover outshines the covered. Still, they'd made her sing the song more than twenty times. He'd lost count after twenty-one, in fact. Dane had no idea why they'd done that, but he trusted the professionals knew more about how to record a hit song than he did. And, he suspected the producer might have been punishing her a little for her less-than-polite attitude toward him.

When he came back out of the bathroom, shirtless, Maggie was just coming through the front door.

She gasped when she saw him.

"What are you doing?" he barked.

She jumped back. "What?"

"Why were you outside?"

"Oh, I just needed something out of the truck."

"You can't go outside without me!" He didn't like how loud his own voice was. He shouldn't be hollering at a woman, or at his boss, or at a woman who was his boss.

She giggled, and even though he was furious with her, it was a cute giggle. "Dane, I just went to the truck. It's like ten feet away."

"I don't care!" he said, still sounding gruffer than he wanted to. He realized he was clenching his fists and forced himself to unfold his fingers. "I wouldn't even have known you were gone. I thought you were still in bed."

"You were in the shower!" she cried, finding some anger of her own. "I'm supposed to wait for you to get out of the shower so I can ask permission to go to my own truck?"

"Yes!" he cried. "That's exactly what you're supposed to do!"

She stared at him with wide, beautiful eyes.

Silence stretched out between them.

"Could you put a shirt on?" she cried, indignant.

He looked down at his bare chest. Oh yeah. He'd forgotten that he was half-dressed. "Stay inside," he said, and stepped into his room, shutting the door behind him.

As he quickly made himself presentable, he strained his ears to hear if she was staying put or walking away. He didn't hear anything; he figured this was a good sign. As quickly as he could, he opened his door again to find her standing right where he'd left her with her hands on her hips.

He took a deep breath. "Sorry that I raised my voice."

She raised an eyebrow.

"But it is my job to protect you, and if you want me to do my job, you have to *let* me protect you."

She nodded. Just barely. "Okay. I'm sorry too."

"Good. A truce then. So, what did you need out of the truck?"

"Oh, just a phone number from an amazing drummer I met a few days ago. I had invited him to the party, but then I forgot to give him the add—"

"What party?" His words came out flat and fast.

"Oh shoot." She bit her bottom lip.

"What party?" he said again.

"I forgot to tell you?" A statement that came up at the end like a question.

Just for a second, he scanned his brain to make sure he *hadn't* forgotten about a party. But no, he had his issues, but blacking out party plans was not one of them. "No. You didn't tell me. And you haven't given me your schedule yet."

"Oh yeah," she said, sounding like a total space cadet.

"What party?" he asked, for what he hoped was the last time.

"So, um ... my new video drops tomorrow, and so tonight there's a party."

He held his hand out. "Where, when, and guest list."

Her eyes widened a bit. "I don't really have a guest list. I've invited all kinds of people."

It was no use continuing to hold his hand out for a list that didn't exist, so he rubbed the back of his head hard enough to hurt. "How are you going to know who to let in if you don't have a guest list?"

At first, she didn't answer, but then he looked at her and tried to pry the explanation out of her with his eyes.

She shrugged. "Nobody knows where it is except the people I invited."

He forced himself to take a breath. "You may be underestimating your letter writer." Fear registered on her face, and he felt bad. He held up one hand. "It's okay, we can fix this. Where's the party?"

"The Tomorrow Club."

"What time?"

"Eight."

He blew out a puff of air. Good. That gave him a little time at least. "Come with me." He led her to the bar in her kitchen and pulled out a stool for her. He grabbed a pen and handed it to her. "Where is the closest paper?"

She pointed with her chin toward her printer.

He fetched a blank piece of paper and put it in front of her. "Do not move until you have written down every single name you can think of that you've invited."

Her eyes widened, and she opened her mouth to argue, but he didn't let her.

"If someone shows up who isn't on the list, they will have to check with you to get in. So try to be thorough."

"But Dane," she said, and he liked the way his name sounded in her voice. "I've invited a *lot* of people."

"Then you'd better get started," he said. She chewed on her pen for a few seconds before writing the first name on the list: Blayze Balin. Dane's stomach rolled, and he didn't know why.

# 13

The club was filling up fast, and Maggie did her best to smile through the pain her stilettos were causing. She was already on her second glass of champagne, and that seemed to be helping to numb the pain as she accepted hugs and shook hands. She saw Dane coming toward her with a sense of urgency. He looked incredibly dashing in his black suit and electric blue dress shirt. She forced herself to look at his eyes. "What?"

"There's a woman named Bessie Wall-Wilcox at the door." He raised one handsome eyebrow as if to suggest that was a ridiculous name.

Maggie giggled and waved a hand. "Yeah, that's just old Bessie. She was a widow and when she remarried, she kept her first married name and just tacked on the new name too." She leaned toward Dane and was almost overpowered by the scent of fir tree. "She's a little weird."

The corner of Dane's lip flickered in the world's fastest smile. "I believe the polite word is eccentric, and I don't need to know her marital history. I need to know if you invited her."

Maggie frowned. As a matter of fact, she didn't think she *had* invited her. Why would she do that? Sure, they'd been like family back when Maggie was in Texas. But Bessie still lived *in Texas*. Why would Maggie invite her to a party in Nashville?

Dane's posture stiffened, and Maggie read his mind. A laugh erupted out of her. "I assure you—Bessie is *not* a threat. She's just a little old lady."

"That you didn't invite."

True. "Maybe my mother invited her."

"You invited your *mother*?" Dane looked horrified.

"Of course I did. She's my *mother.*"

"But she's not on your list."

"Well, I didn't think she'd *come!*"

Dane looked exasperated, and Maggie found a strange sort of pleasure in that. "I invited my sister too, but I don't expect to see her."

"But not your brother?"

"You mean my father's mini-me? No, I didn't invite him."

Dane's face softened into compassion, but then his expression morphed into one of suspicion.

"What?" Maggie asked, her voice barely above a whisper.

"Do you think he might be the letter writer?"

Huh. The thought hadn't occurred to her, but it wasn't all that crazy. She mulled it over for a minute. "It's not impossible, but I don't think so. Because I think he's glad I left the band. He doesn't want me back."

"Good." Dane glanced toward the door. "So, you want me to let Mrs. Wall-Wilcox in?"

She nodded, watched him walk away, and then looked for a place to hide. She didn't want to talk to Bessie, and Dane had a point: it was a little freaky that she was there. She turned to look for someone to talk to, and that someone appeared right in her path: Blayze Balin, larger than life. He was dressed in black from head to toe and had a five o'clock shadow to match.

"Well, look at you, gorgeous," he said, wrapping his arms around her and squeezing too hard.

He smelled like perfume, and she couldn't wait for him to let her go, yet, when he did, she smiled up at him. It would be good for her career to date this guy, no matter how bad he smelled. Things could be worse. At least he was relatively good-looking, though his toothy smile reminded her a little of the wolf that ate Little Red Riding Hood.

"I had an idea about you," she said, trying to layer her voice with honey.

"Oh yeah?" He cocked an eyebrow and put a hand on her hip. "I've had ideas about you too."

She forced a giggle as she playfully removed his hand. "Not *that* kind of idea. Do you know that old song by Rodney Crowell and Rosanne Cash, 'It's Such a Small World'?"

He frowned. "No, why?"

She lost half the respect she had for him right then and there, but she tried not to let that show. "Because it's a great song, and I want to sing it with you. We can put it on my new album, and we can sing it on tour."

His face perked up. "Really?"

"Really. I think you'll like it."

He returned his paw to her hip. "I think I'll like singing *anything* with you, sugar."

Dane appeared over his shoulder, a grimace on his face. "Everything all right, Maggie?"

Blayze's hand was suddenly scorching a hole through her dress, and she sashayed away from him. "Yes. Fine. Everything okay with Bessie?"

"Yes. And she brought a friend. Your mother's here."

# 14

Dane felt like he was caught in a soap opera, and it was exhausting. He hoped that following Maggie around wouldn't always be like this, but he feared that this hope would not be realized.

Looking at Serena Hammer, he could see where Maggie got her beauty. The woman seemed ageless and moved with grace and dignity. The thought of anyone abusing her made his blood run hot. The mysterious Bessie woman trailed behind Serena as she approached her daughter.

Maggie had tears in her eyes as she opened her arms to receive her mother's embrace.

Dane stepped closer to them, just in case, but it seemed to be an ordinary, heartfelt mother and daughter hug.

"Thanks so much for coming, Mom," Maggie whispered into her mother's hair.

Serena stepped back from her daughter, but kept her hands on her arms. "I think you know that I *hate* this new video that we're celebrating tonight, but I love my daughter, and want to support you, even when we disagree."

Dane was impressed. Maggie may have gotten the beauty gene from her mom, but the graciousness gene must have skipped right over her. He also wondered what was so hateable about the new music video.

"Can we talk?" Serena asked softly.

Bessie's eyes were wide as she looked around the dimly lit club. She looked remarkably uncomfortable, and rocked her weight from foot to foot as if preparing to run at the sound of gunfire. Dane had a sudden urge to pull his gun out of its holster and fire at the ceiling, just to see what would happen.

Maggie glanced at Dane as if for permission, but then said, "Sure." She looked around the club, but there didn't seem to be anywhere private to go. "We can go to my dressing room."

The women started walking, and Dane followed closely behind. Serena looked over her shoulder at him, her eyes questioning. "Who is this?"

"He's my bodyguard. Dane, this is my mom, the famous Serena Hammer. Mom, this is Dane." He thought he heard some sarcasm on the word "famous," but Serena either didn't hear it or didn't care. He figured that by now, Serena might be immune to her daughter's sarcasm.

"This is the devil's den," Bessie whispered so quietly Dane wondered if he'd imagined it, but then Serena severely shushed her, confirming that Bessie had, in fact, made that bizarre statement. Dane had been to a few devil's dens in his time. The Tomorrow Club wasn't one of them. It was a clean, reputable venue.

He followed the women into the dressing room, shut the door behind them, and then stood silently in front of it.

Bessie's narrow eyes examined the couch in the room as if it might have bedbugs, but then she sat down.

Serena didn't. She looked at Dane and said, "Is it really necessary that he be in the room with us?"

"Yes," Maggie said quickly, though he thought her insistence to his presence was more about defying her mother than ensuring her safety. "He stays."

*You should tell her about the letters*, Dane thought, but he stayed quiet.

Finally, Serena joined Bessie on the couch, and Maggie sat in a swivel chair facing them. "What do you want to talk about?" Maggie asked, her words clipped.

Pain was etched across Serena's face. "I miss you, honey."

Maggie's chest rose and fell with a quick breath. It seemed she was struggling to breathe. Dane knew that feeling, but was surprised to see it happening to Maggie, and under these circumstances.

"I miss you too, Mom, but you can come see me anytime you want."

"You know I'm busy touring, honey, and taking care of your brother and sister. I can't be chasing you around Nashville."

Maggie avoided her gaze and rested her eyes on Bessie. "And what brings Sister Bessie here?"

Serena cast Bessie a smile. "I asked her to come. She's been my prayer partner in all this."

Maggie rolled her eyes. "And what have you been praying for, exactly?"

"That you would come back to us—"

"I am *never* coming back to the family band, Mom. I am a solo artist now. You need to accept that."

Serena took a deep breath. "Do I? Do I really need to accept that? Because we're not The Hammer Family without you, and I'm not sure how long we'll last—"

Maggie leaned away from her mother abruptly, and the force of her movement slid her chair back a few inches. "Is that what this is about?" she said, almost shrieking. "You're worried about the band not making it?"

Serena shook her head slightly. "Album and single sales are down, and Evelyn doesn't seem as excited about us as they were. Honey, you were part of what made us good."

"I am *totally* what made you good!"

Dane thought this might be an exaggeration.

"And if you'd let me have *any* say in *any* part of the band, maybe I would've stayed."

Dane didn't think this was true either.

"But you kept treating me like a little kid, like I don't know anything about music, about this business—"

"So you wanted to do things your way?" Serena asked, in a distinctly motherly tone.

"Yes!" This time, Maggie did shriek.

"And your way includes you wearing nothing but painted on tiger stripes, crawling around on all fours?!"

*What?* Was that a reference to the music video? If so, what kind of music video *was* it?

Bessie shuddered.

"You make it sound like I'm naked in the video, and I'm not. Don't be so dramatic, Mom."

Dane almost laughed at the irony of that imperative. He was staring directly at the dramatic pot and the equally dramatic kettle, watching them squabble.

"My music is *art*. The video is *art*. And I needed to declare to the world that I am my own person. I needed my own artistic identity—"

"And you certainly got it!" Serena snapped. "So your identity is that you're a wild animal?"

Maggie closed her eyes. "So you didn't come here because you love me and you want to support me. You came here to scold me for making a tiger video?"

"And for singing a song called 'Wild Child.' Are you kidding me? Do you know how that makes your family look?"

Maggie stood so quickly, the chair flew out behind her and crashed into the wall. Red-faced, she pointed at the door. "Get out!" she screamed.

Dane took a step closer.

"Get out now, and take your prayer partner with you! And don't come near me until you're ready to respect me!"

Dane had never heard a voice so high-pitched.

Serena stood and faced her. "Respect?!" she screamed. Okay, *that* was the highest-pitched voice he'd ever heard. He was glad there were no windows in the room, because they might have shattered. "You want to talk to me about respect?" She stepped closer to her daughter, who didn't recoil. They stood nose to nose, with Bessie looking up at them, her eyes wide. "You don't know the first thing about respect! Honor your parents! Now, that's respect!"

Maggie slowly shook her head and dropped her voice by several decibels and at least two octaves. "There is nothing honorable about my parents," she hissed.

That did it. Serena's face recoiled as if she'd been slapped, which in a way, she had been. She stepped back from her daughter, her heel bumping into the couch.

Maggie stepped closer, and Dane feared Serena was going to fall backward onto the couch. "Our family's reputation is a lie, and you know it. Now get out of my face before I tell the whole world the truth."

# 15

Maggie watched the women walk through her dressing room doorway, after Dane opened the door for them with a politeness she found irritating.

Immensely relieved that they were gone, but overwhelmed with guilt, she collapsed onto the couch, leaned her head back, and closed her eyes. What had just happened? Why had she just *let* it happen? What was wrong with her mother? She felt like someone was reaching into her chest and trying to rip her heart out.

"Would you like a minute?" Dane asked softly.

She glanced at the other door to the room, which led to an adjoining dressing room. "Is that safe?" She didn't want him to go anywhere.

"Probably. I can stay right outside. You can holler if you need me."

She allowed herself to look at him, and just the sight of him flooded her with comfort. She didn't think she'd ever felt that particular feeling before, like a wave of peace. It didn't completely relieve the pain in her chest, but it came close. "Nah. You can stay." Then she had another thought. "Unless you *want* to go. I know that was a little crazy." She tried to force a laugh, but it came out flat and fake.

He sat down on the opposite end of the couch, and despite him being a few feet away from her, she could smell the invisible fir needles.

"I'm sorry," he said. "That can't be easy."

She shrugged. She didn't know what to say. "It's not a big deal, really. She just knows how to push my buttons."

"Really? It looked like a big deal to me."

*I wish he would wrap one of those big Christmasy arms around me and pull me into that big chest. I bet he is so warm*—wait. Where did that thought come from? Maybe she was more upset than she thought she was. Either way, she shouldn't be thinking things like that about her bodyguard. She needed to focus on her career right now, and a relationship with Dane wouldn't help her career. It would only distract her from it. Besides, she didn't believe in love, right?

"Would you really air your family's dirty laundry with the press?"

She thought about that for a minute. "I don't think so, but it's the best threat ever. My mother would rather die than have anyone think she had anything less than a perfect little family."

"And your father?" Dane's jaw clenched as he spoke the words. "Is the family's image important to him too?"

She had to think about that one too. Dane was asking difficult questions. "I don't know. It's been a long time since I thought about what was important to him. But if I had to guess, I don't think so. Right now, I think he's just worried about money. He seems to be enjoying having some of it for the first time in his life, and as far as I know, he's been nicer to everyone since the money started coming in. I guess he doesn't want to blow it. So no, I guess I wouldn't go to the press. If fame and money protect my mother from him, then I want her success to continue." She chuckled. "Maybe I should do a duet with her instead of with Blayze."

Dane flinched at the mention of Blayze's name. "What about Bessie? Do you think she's dangerous?"

Maggie laughed. "Bessie? No way." Visions flashed through Maggie's head: Bessie in the front row at church, singing her favorite hymn with her hands in the air; Bessie teaching her in Sunday school; Bessie driving her around to deliver meals to shut-ins when her mother couldn't do it because she had a black eye—"No way," Maggie said again. "Bessie is a saint."

"Saints can be dangerous."

"I'm telling you, don't worry about Bessie."

They were interrupted by a knock on the door. Dane jumped up to open it. A young woman Maggie didn't recognize stuck her head into the room. "Blayze is on stage and he's asking for you."

*What?* Maggie frowned. "He's asking for *me*? Are you sure?"

The girl nodded, looking like she had somewhere else to be. "I guess he wants you to sing with him?"

Maggie jumped up and smoothed out her skirt. She hadn't planned on performing, but performing was probably just what she needed. She never felt better, more comfortable, more confident than when she was on stage. "I'll be right there." She looked at Dane. "Here goes nothing." And she led the way back out into the crowded club and toward the stage, aware of his strong presence right behind her. She walked by a server holding a tray full of champagne flutes and paused to pour a glass of bubbly down her throat. She wasn't much of a drinker and didn't even know why the urge had hit her tonight, but she was an adult, and she could do what she pleased. Just before she reached the stage, she veered to the right to pass another server and have herself a second glass. She was already in a better mood, already felt warmer and happier, when she stepped on stage and gave Blayze her most dazzling smile. "What are we doing, sugar?" She asked, making sure to speak loudly enough so that the microphone would pick her up.

"Well, sugar," Blayze said with a smile that matched or exceeded the dazzle of her own, "I thought we could debut our duet."

Her smile almost faltered. She leaned closer to him and lowered her voice. "I thought you didn't know it?"

"I said that twenty minutes ago. Then I went out back and learned it. Now I know it."

She found that hard to believe. How could anyone learn a song in twenty minutes? And he had his electric guitar. So not only was he going to sing it, he was going to play it? This was going to be a disaster. What had she been thinking joining forces with this unprofessional nincompoop? She tried to think of a way out, but the buzz in her brain was telling her it would be fine, not to worry about it. Should she pretend to have a cold? Or was there another song he knew better? What song did they both know? She looked out at the crowd, and stood there frozen, a foolish smile plastered across her face. But he didn't wait for her to form an escape plan. Before she even knew what was happening, he was playing the opening guitar riff, and it was so on point that her whole body broke out in gooseflesh. She was transported into a different realm, and transformed into the stage persona that was the up-and-coming superstar Maggie Hammer. Right on cue, Blayze sang the first words, and Maggie knew they had a smash hit on their hands. A hush fell over the crowd. Her eyes scanned the room. Most people didn't recognize the song yet, and that was okay. They would soon enough. But plenty of people did know it. Several were singing along and many wore broad smiles that could only mean one thing: they already knew and loved the song. Sometimes old-timers got snotty when newcomers covered songs—she hadn't even been born when the original was recorded—but she didn't see a hint of that anywhere. Although, in theory, this should be a room full of her people, so she hoped none of them would be snotty—especially now that her mother had left.

She let her body move to the music and didn't think she'd ever been so happy. Though, when Blayze sang the lyrics that told her she looked good, he moved his eyes up and down her body in a way that made her feel slightly violated. She pushed that away and got ready to fully enter the song. He nodded to her, as if she didn't know when to come in, as if *she* was the one who hadn't known the song twenty minutes ago, and with the confidence of a thousand angels, she stepped up to the mic and unleashed the power of her throaty alto. She gazed out into the crowd and could see that they were eating it up, and she gave them her all.

Blayze came back in, right on cue, and then she joined him when he got to the song's hook, harmonizing with him, and knowing their voices were melding into something synergistically powerful. The man was a natural. She had underestimated his talent, his gift. Maybe he was more than just a handsome face and tight jeans. Maybe she hadn't been wrong to invite this nincompoop onto her tour.

He stopped singing and, with enviable showmanship, gave her people a guitar solo that would impress even the best. She knew they would need some piano for the real deal, but for now, what they were doing was enough to make people happy. In this moment, *she* was enough—and that was a feeling she didn't get to enjoy very often.

# 16

D ane was miserable, and he didn't even know why. He knew he had a habit of seeing danger everywhere, even when there wasn't any, but he also knew that there was usually danger that most people couldn't see. He knew, beyond a shadow of a doubt, that Blayze was dangerous. He didn't want Maggie on stage with him, he didn't want her on tour with him, he didn't want her anywhere near him. But obviously, he was not in control. And he didn't like it. He didn't like watching Maggie rub her body against a man who might very well be just like her father.

Still, he had to admit they were killing it. He didn't know the song, but he didn't have to know it to know they were doing it well. The crowd looked mesmerized. He scanned the faces looking for anyone out of place, anyone unhappy, or anyone who looked as though they could pose a threat. But with creepy Bessie gone, the only person in the whole room who put his hackles up was the man on stage. In fact, the more the song went on, the more anxious Dane got. And it seemed to be the longest song in the history of songs. He counted the seconds for it to be over, and hoped against hope that they wouldn't sing another.

He couldn't stand the way Maggie was looking at Blayze, all sensual and sassy. He knew she was just performing—at least he thought she was. And he didn't know why her on-stage flirting would even bother him. He chalked it up to his primal dislike of the man, telling himself that if she was flirting with a different performer, then he wouldn't mind.

At long last, they sang the final note in perfect harmony, and Dane let out a long breath. The crowd went crazy, and Maggie stepped off the front of the stage right into the thick of it, instead of using the steps on the side of the stage. As her high-heeled foot hit the floor, her ankle rolled beneath her, and she let out a cry of pain. He was there in a second, but he still didn't beat Blayze, who jumped off the stage like a teen-aged athlete and scooped her up in his arms.

"Get your hands off her," Dane said, before he could think about it.

Blayze sneered at him and made no effort to let go of her. Instead, he looked down at her and said, "Are you all right?"

Maggie's eyes swam with tears. Dane took her free hand, the one that wasn't wrapped around Blayze, and said, "Let's get you out of here."

She shook her head. "No, no, I'm okay." She looked around the room, which was full of silent, concerned faces, and snapped her fingers at one of the servers holding a tray of drinks. "I just need some liquid painkiller."

The audience erupted in what sounded like relieved laughter as the server approached. To Dane's dismay, she let go of him to grab a glass of champagne. But the good news was, she also let go of Blayze to grab another. So, with tears falling and all her weight on one foot, she held one glass in the air and called out, "Cheers!"

The crowd laughed again. The crowd was starting to annoy him immensely.

Blayze let go of her then and looked at Dane. They stood eye to eye. Dane didn't like that. He preferred to be taller than someone he was trying to stare down. "She's fine," Blayze said.

Dane ignored that and kept one hand on the small of her back.

She put one empty glass back on the tray and grabbed another full one.

He was desperate to tell her to slow down, but knew it wasn't his place. He needed to get her away from these people if he was going to say something like that. "Let's find you a seat?" Had she eaten anything tonight? He really hoped so.

She smiled up at him, but there was no joy in her eyes. "Just a second." She downed the drink, returned the glass to the tray, and then slid her empty hand into his. Her hand felt cool and small, and his heart swelled, desperate to protect her. She leaned toward him and whispered, "Yeah, let's sit down."

He tried to lead her to the back of the room where couches lined the wall, but people kept stopping to tell her how much they loved the song, how much she sounded like Rosanne Cash, how proud Rosanne and Rodney would be of that performance. People wanted to know when the single would be released, when they could download it, would it be on the current album? Maggie deftly and charmingly dodged each of these questions as she inched her way to the back of the room, fully leaning on Dane's hand. Her hand trembled in his, and he wondered how she could remain so charismatic while in so much pain. She was playing a character and doing it well.

Finally, they reached the back wall, and she collapsed onto a leather sofa. Dane was grateful that people had decided to give her some space and he knelt in front of her and picked up her foot. Her ankle was the size of a softball. "We need to get this x-rayed."

She laughed. "Nah, I just need more champagne."

He tried to keep his voice even. "You go on tour in a week. You need medical attention. Getting drunker isn't going to help anything."

She laughed so hard she snorted. "Drunker? Is that even a word?" She patted the seat beside her. "Can't we just relax for a minute?" She sounded out of breath. She put her elbow on the armrest, leaned her head onto it, and closed her eyes.

He sat beside her and leaned toward her.

"Mmm ... You smell good."

That bizarre compliment had more of an effect on him than it should have, but he tried to ignore the butterflies in his stomach. "Please, Maggie, let me take you to the hospital."

"You smell like Christmas."

He didn't know what that meant, but he thought it was probably the nicest thing anyone had ever said about him.

# 17

Maggie's ankle was throbbing, and the room was spinning. Wasn't alcohol supposed to get rid of pain? She shuddered to think how badly her ankle would hurt if she *hadn't* had oodles of bubbly. She looked at Dane, who was sitting blessedly close to her. "How much champagne is too much champagne?" The second time she spoke the word, she thought maybe she slurred it. She wouldn't testify to that in court, though.

He chuckled, but it was humorless, and he didn't answer her, which annoyed her. She saw her manager, Andre, approaching. As he dropped down onto the couch beside her, Dane slid out of the way. She'd never been so mad at Andre. It had been *so* obvious that there was no room on that sofa for a third party. "Haven't you ever heard that three's a crowd?" she mumbled, but he acted as though he didn't hear her. Maybe he didn't.

"That was spectacular!" he cried. She could see the dollar signs in his eyes.

"Thanks."

"No, really! You seemed to bring something out of Blayze Balin that I hadn't seen before." He paused, then blurted out, "Talent!" and laughed at his own joke.

This was absurd. Blayze had all the talent in the world. Andre just hadn't been paying attention.

"For the first time, I see that it's a good idea to bring him on tour!"

Maggie couldn't see Dane, but she could sense him grimacing at that statement. She didn't know why he disliked Blayze so much, but it was obvious that he did. Maybe he just saw him as a threat—which

Maggie didn't. Blayze wasn't a choirboy. He was probably a womanizer. But he wasn't dangerous. At least, she didn't think so.

"We've got to get the go-ahead to record these songs, so I'll keep after them to give it. And I think you should put that duet on your album."

Maggie nodded. She'd already planned on that and was tired of talking to Andre. She wanted him to move so she could look at Dane some more. But before she could get rid of Andre, Blayze approached the couch. If three was a crowd, what was four? She was suddenly very tired.

Blayze held out a hand. "Wanna dance?"

She shook her head, ignoring his outstretched hand. "No thanks. I think I've had too much to drink."

Blayze laughed. "No such thing." He reached down, grabbed her hand off her lap, and pulled her to her feet. She wobbled, but he caught her. "I'll hold you up." He wrapped an arm around her waist. She started to look at Dane, but Blayze pulled her body into his and she couldn't help but look at him instead. His body was warm and made her sleepier. He started to pull her onto the dance floor, and vaguely, she wondered if Dane was following them.

"Wait!" she said, and he stopped, though he seemed reluctant.

She kicked off her shoes, flipping them back toward the couch, but when she kicked off her second shoe, a nauseating pain raced up her leg. She cried out and started to fall. Blayze caught her around the waist, but then a second pair of arms scooped her entirely off the floor. Without looking, she knew they were Dane's arms, and she was so glad. "I think I'm gonna be sick," she mumbled.

"I know."

Before she realized what was happening, Dane was kicking open the door to the women's restroom, and carrying her through it. She found this hysterical and started to giggle, but then the smell of the bathroom hit her and she retched. Dane got her to the toilet just in time, and the champagne left her body with a desperate enthusiasm. Dane held her hair back for her, and she was grateful, as it had taken an hour to get it the way she wanted.

It didn't take long, and when she finished, she tried to sit on the floor, but Dane wouldn't let her. He scooped her back up in his tree trunk arms, flushed with his foot, and said, "Now we go to the hospital."

She nestled her head into his Christmasy chest and didn't care where he took her, as long as she could stay right there in that warm, wonderful-smelling spot.

# 18

D ane wasn't glad that Maggie was in pain, but he was grateful for an excuse to leave the club, and that irritating Blayze behind. What kind of name was Blayze, anyway? And even if some hippie mother *had* named her baby boy Blayze, surely she wouldn't have spelled it with a y? No, he was almost certain that arrogant nut had named him*self* Blayze, and Dane couldn't believe the deed hadn't harmed his career more than it had. He was dying to know what the guy's name really was. Probably Alfred. Or Rudolph. Or Kermit. He hoped it was something even worse, something so bad he couldn't think of it right now.

He tucked Maggie into the backseat of her SUV; if she got sick again, he didn't want to deal with that in the front. He didn't think she would, though. She'd done a pretty thorough job of emptying herself out in the restroom. He was annoyed with her drunkenness, but it was also obvious to him that this didn't happen much. A seasoned drinker wouldn't have allowed herself to drink so much, so fast, at least not at a party thrown in her professional honor. At least not a seasoned drinker who cared as much about her image as Maggie Hammer did.

She stirred as he buckled her in, and without opening her eyes, reached up and ran her fingers through his hair. His entire body broke out in goosebumps, and he felt guilty, even though he hadn't done anything wrong. "That's enough of that," he said, gently returning her hand to her lap, where it belonged.

As he started to get into the driver's seat, Andre trotted up beside him. "What's going on?"

Dane just looked at him. What did that question even mean?

"It's not even ten o'clock yet."

Dane glanced at Maggie through the window. "She's asleep."

"She wasn't asleep five minutes ago," Andre snapped, as though Dane had forced her to snack on some sleeping pills.

Further interaction with this man was not going to be worth it, so Dane got into the truck and shut the door. Andre knocked on his window, which was a ridiculous gesture. It wasn't like he didn't know he was there. "Where are you taking her?" Andre asked with more volume than necessary, but Dane just put the truck in reverse and backed out of the parking spot, leaving an open-mouthed Andre behind.

Not for long, though. Dane hadn't driven a mile before he saw that he was being followed. His first thought was the letter-writer, but then he thought a more reasonable theory was that Andre had given chase. Sure enough, the sedan followed him into the parking lot, and Andre crawled out. Dane liked him less and less every minute. Would he like *anyone* in Maggie's life? He really wasn't that hard to please, but so far, it seemed Maggie was surrounded by increasingly obnoxious individuals. At this point, his favorite was Bessie Wall-Wilcox.

"What are we doing here?" Andre cried.

Dane opened the back door, and Maggie picked her head up.

"Hi," he said softly. "We're at the hospital. Let's go get that ankle x-rayed."

She nodded, seeming soberer than the last time he'd tried to communicate with her. "It really hurts."

"I'm sure it does. Want me to carry you?"

She seemed to internally debate that for a moment, but then shook her head. "Nah." She slid out of the car, landing on her good foot, which was still bare. Shoot. Her shoes were still up front.

"*May* I carry you?" he asked, trying to emphasize that he wanted to.

"Nah," she said again, but put her arm around his shoulder as she shut the SUV's door behind them.

"Let me grab your shoes then." He opened the front door and grabbed the heels. He slid one onto her good foot. She was a modern-day Cinderella, and he was both her prince and her pumpkin-driver.

"Actually, I'd rather be barefoot. Thanks anyway."

Okay, not the prince. Just the pumpkin-driver. He tossed the shoes back into the vehicle and shut the door.

She seemed to notice Andre for the first time. "You didn't have to come."

Andre looked exasperated. "Well, you can be sure no one invited me." He threw a dirty look in Dane's direction. It had no effect. "I didn't even know you were injured."

How could he not know she was injured? Everyone in the club had seen her fall off the stage!

Maggie started to hop toward the front door.

"Please, let me carry you."

"It's okay. I'm a Texan."

And despite the situation, Dane had to laugh at that. Then his guilty smile turned into one of real joy when a man in scrubs came trotting toward them pushing a wheelchair.

"Wait." Dane halted Maggie's forward progress, and she paused, leaning all her weight into him.

"Thank you," Maggie said, and collapsed into the chair. Then she looked up at the hospital sign. "What are we doing here?" she cried.

Maybe she was drunker than he thought. "You need to get your ankle looked at," he explained again.

"No!" She glared at him. "I mean, why are we at *this* hospital?"

Dane looked up at the sign, confused.

Maggie explained herself—loudly enough for anyone in the parking lot or sleeping on the first floor to hear. "Artists don't come *here*! Stop!" The man in scrubs stopped, mere feet from the door. Maggie pushed herself up and tried to stomp back toward the truck, barefoot and limping, but the pain was too much and she stopped and bent over, crying. "Take me to the good hospital!" she screamed at

Dane, and he didn't know what to do. He looked at Andre, who was also glaring at him. Seriously? This mattered?

Okay then, he would obey the wishes of the rich and crazy. Without asking permission this time, he scooped Maggie up and returned her to the backseat, letting her buckle herself in this time. And then, as he climbed into the front, he saw with horror that Andre had inserted himself into the passenger seat. Wow. He silently vowed to ask for a raise soon.

# 19

Maggie couldn't stop crying, and that made her furious with herself, which made the tears flow even faster. The physical pain was brutal, but that was the easiest part. It was much harder to deal with her embarrassment. Who gets so drunk at their own party that they fall off a stage? Even the artists who drank all the time and got arrested for being fools in public didn't fall off their stages. She didn't even know it was possible to get that drunk off champagne. And she hadn't even had very much! And then there was the fear. The overwhelming fear that she was going to start her tour on crutches. Would they even do that? Or would they make her postpone her shows? Or worse, cancel shows? How was she going to twitch her hips seductively with a cast on one foot? It was these overpowering emotions that had made her lash out at Dane in the parking lot like some sort of psychotic diva. Why had she done that? Why couldn't she have just gone to the closest hospital like a normal person? She hadn't meant to holler at Dane. Now she felt horrible for it. He had been so kind, so nonjudgmental, through this whole thing. She kept her head down so that neither of the men in the front could see how emotional she was. Andre prattled on and on about things she knew Dane didn't care about. She didn't even know why Andre was there. He didn't care about her health or well-being. *He's just worried about the tour.* Once the thought occurred to her, she knew it was true.

Her phone buzzed, and she looked around for her purse.

Wordlessly, Dane handed it back to her over the front seat.

"Why do you have my purse?" As soon as she finished the question, she cringed at the snippiness in her own voice. Why did she continue to be so mean to him? He didn't answer her. It had been a stupid question anyway. He'd obviously grabbed it before they'd left the party. She couldn't even clearly remember leaving the club. She just remembered starting to dance, then falling, then Dane carrying her, and then her getting sick. A new wave of embarrassment flooded over her. How many people had seen her being carried into the bathroom? How many had seen her being carried out of her own party? How many pictures had been taken? She tried to tell herself that there was no such thing as bad publicity, but she wasn't convinced. She was trying to convey to the world that she was a grownup. But grownups knew how to drink champagne.

She tapped the text message icon and saw a message from Blayze. "Are you okay?"

She tipped her head back and closed her eyes. She didn't want to answer him right now, didn't trust herself to put anything into writing. But it was sweet that he cared. Then she realized that he too was probably worried about the tour. That meant that *everybody* was just worried about the tour. No one was worried about her.

"Stop the car!" she cried before she even realized she was speaking.

Dane looked at her in the rearview but did not apply the brakes.

"Stop the car!" she screamed.

Dane pulled the car over to the shoulder. "Are you going to be sick—"

She didn't let him finish his question. Andre turned and looked at her. She looked back at him. "Get out!"

Andre laughed at her and turned to face front.

Her blood was boiling. "Get out of my car!" she said, with more volume this time.

"No." Andre said in an even tone that sounded almost sinister.

"Get out of my car now! I did not invite you on this errand and I don't want you here. Get out!" She knew she sounded completely unhinged but she didn't care.

Andre waved his arm toward the darkness outside. "I'm not getting out *here*, Maggie. Sober up."

Maggie considered reaching around his headrest with both hands and clawing his eyes out, but she didn't want to go to jail.

"I believe the owner of this vehicle asked you to step out of the vehicle," Dane said in a level voice, and Maggie wanted to kiss the back of his head.

"You've got to be kidding me." For the first time, Andre sounded as though he believed he might have to exit the vehicle.

"Do you need some help?" Dane asked.

Andre turned to look at Maggie. "If I get out, we are *done*."

Maggie wasn't sure if that was true, and started to waver on her conviction of getting him out of her car. It wasn't easy to find a manager in a city where everyone hated you for abandoning your perfect, precious mother. But she couldn't back down. Not now. "Get out."

Andre looked at Dane one more time, incredulous, but Dane stared straight ahead. Finally, Andre got out of the truck. As soon as the door slammed shut behind him, Dane looked in the rearview, and the two of them locked eyes. "Are you sure?" he asked softly.

"I'm sure."

Dane moved his turn signal from right to left and eased out into traffic.

## 20

*N*ever going to be a dull moment with this one, Dane thought as he watched Andre shrink away in the rearview mirror. He wondered if Andre would really stop working with her. "Do you have a contract with that guy?"

"Yep. And it's a terrible one. I begged him to work with me."

Dane thought about that. He wished he knew more about the business. "Aren't you going to lose money then, if you break that contract?"

"Don't care. But I don't think so. He's the one who broke the contract, not me."

Dane wasn't sure that what just happened comprised an actual breaking of contract, but time would tell. "Do you know anyone else who would manage you?"

"Nope."

*Poor Maggie.* He didn't exactly agree with her decision to kick her manager out of the truck, but he completely understood why she did it. Sometimes, misery doesn't love company. Sometimes, misery just wants to be left alone. He pulled the vehicle in front of the emergency room doors of the correct hospital and turned the engine off. Someone approached the vehicle immediately. "I can go park your vehicle for you, sir," he said, as another person appeared with a wheelchair.

"Sure. Keys are in the ignition." He got out, keeping a close eye on Maggie, who was already being helped out of the truck and into the wheelchair.

He followed the two of them into the hospital and a brightly lit waiting room. He squinted as his eyes adjusted, and looked around the room, which was crowded. This was going to take a while. He stood a respectful distance behind Maggie as she gave the woman behind the window some information, but he still heard her when she said she didn't have any health insurance. Good grief, this woman was a financial disaster. He might never get paid. Maybe he *wouldn't* ask for a raise just yet.

With clipboard in hand, Maggie turned to look at him. "Can you push me?" She sounded exhausted.

He jumped to push her toward the other waiting patients and wondered how many contagions were in this room. She might start her tour with a broken ankle and a case of whooping cough. He parked her and sat beside her, glancing down at her now-bright-red ankle. "How's your pain?"

"I'm in absolute agony. But I guess I deserve it." He'd never heard her sound so sad, and was desperate to comfort her.

"I wouldn't say that." He had the urge to take her hand, but he resisted it.

"Really?" She looked at him with wide, wet eyes. "You think it was a good idea to drink a bunch of champagne even though I don't know how to drink champagne and then fall off a stage?"

He smiled. "No, I don't think it was a good idea. But life happens to the best of us. Don't beat yourself up." He looked down at her ankle. "Any more than you already have."

She giggled, and it was a beautiful sound.

He rubbed his jaw, trying to think of a way to make conversation and distract her from her pain. "So ... does anyone know Blayze's real name?"

"Sure. It's Bernard Biotrowski."

No way. That was even worse than he'd imagined. "Seriously?"

"Yep. At least, that's what Wikipedia says. I've never discussed it with him."

"I think you should," Dane said, and she tipped her head back and laughed again. Her laughter made his heart dance. He realized then that her happiness really mattered to him. "Anything else I can do for you?"

She looked around the room. "I'm *starving*."

"On it." He jumped up to find a vending machine. "Candy, granola, or crackers?"

She reached into her purse. "I'll take one of each."

He held up a hand. "It's my treat." Trying to keep one eye on her, he headed around the corner to look for a snack machine. He knew there would be better options in the cafeteria, but he didn't want to leave her for that long.

When he returned with a Milky Way Marshmallow bar (he hadn't even known they made such a thing), an organic gluten-free granola bar, and the world's smallest bag of Cheezits, someone was standing too close to and leaning over Maggie. Shoot. He shouldn't have left her. He quickened his pace, but soon realized it was just some fan with bad social skills. Maggie graciously autographed the magazine subscription card he'd ripped out of last month's *People* and gave him a big smile. When Dane got close, the young man scurried away. "Sorry," Dane said, handing her the makeshift meal, "the choices weren't great."

"That's okay." She ripped into the chocolate bar. "This is perfect. Thank you." She closed her eyes as she chewed and seemed to be enjoying the candy a great deal. Oh great. Now he wanted a Milky Way Marshmallow bar too.

His craving was interrupted, however, by a hysterical teenage couple who came tearing into the ER like their pants were on fire. The girl was sobbing—loudly—and held one hand over her ear. The boy trailed her, looking embarrassed—but well-trained. Dane couldn't hear what the woman behind the glass said, but he certainly heard the girl's response. "My stupid ear is infected!" she shouted. Was this infection causing deafness?

The boyfriend stepped closer, sheepishly. "Uh ... actually, it's not the ear, but the earring hole."

No way.

More inaudible speech from behind the glass.

"No!" the girl shrieked. "I need you to take it out!" She paused. "Take it out now!"

"Please, can you help us? She just pierced it today," the boyfriend added.

Dane strained to hear what the professional behind the glass was saying. He was a little embarrassed by how entertaining he found this.

The girl started pounding on the glass with her free hand. "Get it out! Get it out now! It's killing me!"

Without warning, Maggie whirled around. "Sit down and shut up!"

The girl turned on her. "Why don't you mind your own business?!"

Oh dear. As if tonight wasn't already strange enough.

"You going to make me?" Maggie appeared determined to fight this girl.

Suddenly, the girl's expression morphed from fury to curious delight. "Hey, aren't you that Hammer chick?"

Maggie gave her a tight smile. "Yes, I am, and my head is killing me," she said with clipped words, "so I'd be grateful if you'd have a seat and wait quietly like the rest of us."

"I would!" the girl said, her voice rising in volume again as she turned toward the window, "but they're acting like this isn't an emergency! Which it *is!*"

Maggie tipped her head back and closed her eyes, as if it was taking all her strength not to transform into the Hulk. Dane reached over and squeezed her hand. "Take a deep breath. This will all be over soon."

# 21

Maggie could almost feel her blood pressure going down at the touch of Dane's hand. She looked up into his brown eyes and almost felt better. But then the lunatic teenager started pounding and shrieking again.

"Ma'am?" Dane said, standing up. "Maybe I can help."

What? What was he doing? He walked over to the window and asked the woman behind it for a pair of rubber gloves. A moment later, he was putting them on, and he turned to face the girl who still had her hand over her ear.

"You're not a doctor," she said.

He dropped his now-blue hands to his side. "Do you want the thing out or not?"

She stared up at him.

"Don't, Dane," Maggie said, "she'll sue you."

The girl gave Maggie a dirty look.

Dane swept one arm away from the reception window, which newcomers were now trying to reach, some of whom appeared to have actual medical issues. Slowly, he led the distraught couple toward Maggie. "What's your name?" he asked the girl.

"Natalia."

"Hi, Natalia. I'm Dane." He looked at the boy.

"Bob," the boy said.

Dane nodded and looked back to Natalia. "I got first aid training in the service. And I'm willing to help you right now. Want me to take a look?"

Slowly, the girl dropped her hand from her ear, and she nodded.

Dane leaned closer, but Maggie could tell from where she sat that there was nothing wrong with the girl's ear. Sure, it had an earring in it, but it wasn't red or swollen. The expression on Dane's face declared that he was thinking the same thing. He looked at Bob. "You couldn't have pulled this thing out?"

The boy shrugged.

"All right. Hold still." Dane reached behind her ear with one hand, grabbed the earring with the other, and in less than a second, he had pulled the offending earring out of Natalia's ear.

She howled in pain.

Maggie rolled her eyes. This was the most ridiculous thing she'd ever seen in her life—and she'd seen some things.

Dane dropped the earring into Natalia's hand. "Do you want the other one out?"

The girl looked up at him as if she wanted to marry him and have his babies. She nodded.

He stepped to the other side of her and pulled out her other earring. He placed that in her hand too, and then peeled off his rubber gloves.

"Wow, thank you *so* much," she said, still standing in the same place as Dane headed to the trash can.

"Yeah, thanks, man," Bob said.

"Don't mention it."

Then the couple just stood there with irritating cluelessness.

"You can go now," Maggie said, waving toward the door.

Without taking her eyes off Dane, who didn't return her gaze, Natalia led Bob out of the hospital. Maggie had never felt so relieved. She looked at the man beside her. "I can't believe you just did that."

"I did it for you," he said without looking at her.

She giggled. "What? What does that mean?"

He turned toward her. "I was afraid you were going to do something crazy, and I don't have any bail money." He smirked. "And I don't think you do either."

Her cheeks got hot. "Well, then ... thank you. That was so bizarre. There was nothing wrong with her."

"I don't know about that, but her earring hole wasn't infected."

Maggie giggled again. The giggling seemed to ease the pain in her ankle a smidgen. "Maybe the piercing just hurt more than she thought it would?"

Dane opened his mouth to say something, but a nurse from the other side of the room called out Maggie's name. Maggie was disappointed. She would have rather heard what Dane was going to say. Instead, he stood and pushed her toward the swinging doors that the nurse held open.

When he reached the nurse, he took his hands off the chair and said to her, "She can't walk."

Maggie realized then that he didn't plan to go with her. Before she could think about how weird it would be to do so, she grabbed his arm. "Please come with me!"

"There won't be much room back there," the nurse said sternly, making her preference clear.

"I'll be right here," Dane said, looking down at her with an intensity that made her quiver.

Grudgingly, she let go of his arm and allowed the mean nurse to push her down the sterile hallway. How had this night gone so wrong? She wished it were all a bad dream. The nurse shoved her into a small cubicle with an exam table. "The doctor will be right with you." She yanked the flimsy blue curtain shut.

Maggie looked around the small space. There was *plenty* of room for Dane here.

# 22

Several hours after Dane watched Maggie get wheeled away, he watched her come hobbling toward him on crutches with a cast on her foot. His chest filled with joy at the sight of her. Was that because he was growing attached to his new boss or was he just happy at the prospect of getting out of the hospital? He wasn't sure. Either way, he was amazed at how long it took to diagnose and cast an ankle injury. He went toward her, trying not to look too eager. "Well, that was quick."

She laughed, but it sounded tired. She seemed to be struggling to keep her eyes open.

"Is it broken?"

She shook her head. "Maybe broken would've been better. It's a bad sprain, but they're saying I need to wear this thing for weeks." Her voice was deep and shaky. She looked into his eyes. "So, my tour is shot."

"It's not shot," he said quickly, even though he had no idea. "But let's deal with that after you've gotten some sleep. Do you need to check out?"

She took a few wobbly steps. "Nah, they took all my information back there. Let's get out of here before I fall asleep standing up." He let her lead, so relieved they were finally getting on with their night—before it turned to morning. The valet saw him coming and left to get their vehicle. Dane followed Maggie and him out into the fresh night air, which felt nearly miraculous on his face. He'd spent a great deal of his life in that waiting room. He expected Maggie to stop and wait for her vehicle, but she made a beeline for a stone bench in the shadows. As he watched her go, he noticed a little boy sitting on the bench. What on earth? He looked around in the darkness, but didn't see any adults. Why was a parentless child sitting on a hospital's bench in the middle of the night?

Maggie wordlessly sat down beside him and held up her hand to stop Dane from approaching. What was she doing? Just sitting there? There were other benches closer to the door, and she hadn't sat down on them, so it wasn't just that she was resting.

Maggie's SUV pulled up in front of the doors they were now nowhere near. "Uh, Maggie?"

She held up the hand again, which he was starting to find patronizing.

"Your truck's here."

"Can you go park it?" she snapped.

He liked Maggie, he really did, but he was reaching his limit, and no, he wasn't going to leave her, injured and exhausted, sitting with a strange kid in the dark. Walking mostly backward, he returned to the valet and apologized, explaining that apparently, they weren't quite ready to go yet. Dane tipped him a few of his last dollars, but the valet didn't blink, leading Dane to think that this was far from the strangest thing he'd had to do tonight. He had probably also met the earring couple.

By the time Dane returned to Maggie and child, she had him talking. At least, his lips were moving.

"Michael's a great name," Maggie said. "I had a cat named Michael once. He was really good at catching mice."

The little boy, presumably named Michael, laughed. His cheeks were wet. Dane's impatient heart softened, in part because of the kid, and in part because of Maggie's heart for the kid.

"Also, did you know there's an angel named Michael?"

Wide-eyed, Michael shook his head.

"Oh, yeah," Maggie said slowly and dramatically, "Michael is an archangel. That means he's one of the most powerful angels in the universe—maybe *the most* powerful! He commands God's army of angels! No bad guy wants to mess with him!" She seemed to notice Dane then and gave him a small smile. He took a short step closer, not because he thought she needed his protection, but just because he wanted to better hear their conversation. She looked at Michael. "Do you know any bad guys?"

Michael shrugged.

"Maybe?"

He nodded.

"Are you in danger right now?"

He shrugged again.

"Maybe?"

"I don't know," he said softly.

Maggie dramatically let out a great breath and tipped her head back. "Oh, thank the heavens! That probably means you're not in danger then."

Dane wasn't sure, but he thought Michael looked encouraged by that.

"Okay then," Maggie said. "I'm glad you're not in danger, but it's not safe for anyone to sit out here in the dark in the middle of the night. So, do you want to go home?" She eyed him closely.

He didn't answer her.

"Yeah, I know what you mean. Sometimes I don't want to go home either. Is there someplace you *do* want to go?"

He thought about it and then nodded eagerly.

"Oh yeah? Where?"

"Grammy's house!"

Maggie gave him a broad smile. "That's an excellent idea! What's your Grammy's name?"

He looked confused. To him, Grammy's name was Grammy. "Uh ... Alice."

"Oh, that's a pretty name. But it's not an angel's name!" She laughed, and Michael joined her.

"Yeah," he agreed.

"At least, I don't think it is. I've never met an angel named Alice. I suppose it's possible, though."

Michael's eyes widened. "You've met an angel before?"

Maggie nodded, her brow furrowed to convey her sincerity. "Oh yes." She swept her hand out toward the dark lawn. "There are angels everywhere. Usually we can't see them, but they're here."

Michael's eyes followed her arm, and he stared into the darkness. He looked convinced. Maggie could be very persuasive.

"So, what's Grammy's last name?"

He thought for another minute, and Dane thought he wasn't going to come up with it. Then he said, "Turner."

"Is that your last name too?"

He nodded.

Maggie looked disappointed. At first, Dane didn't know why, but then he figured "Turner" might just be a guess. Maybe the kid assumed his grandmother would have the same last name as him.

"Is this your mom's mom or your dad's mom?"

"Mom's mom," Michael said quickly, and then laughed, presumably at how it sounded to say that out loud.

"Great. Do you think I could meet your Grammy?"

He shrugged.

"Do you know her phone number?"

He shook his head.

Dane's stomach sank, but Maggie was undeterred. "That's okay. Does your Grammy have a job?"

Michael thought for a minute and then nodded. "She's a waitress."

"Oh!" Maggie said, back to being dramatic. "Waitresses are the best! They bring you food!"

Michael giggled.

"Do you know what restaurant she works at?"

He shook his head, but then his face brightened. "She works by the airport! Planes fly over her restaurant. They're loud!"

"Does she work by the Nashville airport?"

He looked confused.

"Is it a short ride to go see her or a long ride?"

Michael shrugged again. The kid sure was a shrugger.

"Does it take four songs on the radio to get to her or twenty songs?"

Michael scrunched up his face as he did the calculations in this head. "Four."

"Okay great. So, I have an idea. Are you hungry?"

He nodded quickly.

Maggie finally looked at Dane. "This here is my friend, Dane. How about if he and I take you to the airport? Do you think you could recognize the restaurant if you saw it?"

Michael didn't look so sure.

Dane was certain this was a bad idea. You don't put a strange lost kid into your vehicle and drive around looking for a needle in a haystack. "Uh, Maggie, could I talk to you?"

She ignored him. "Well, if you recognize the restaurant, then we'll get something to eat. And if you don't recognize the restaurant, we'll still pick a restaurant—"

"Maggie, they're not going to be open," Dane tried.

She glared at him. "Can you get the truck, please?"

Dane took a deep breath and returned to the valet. This was such a terrible idea. How could he make her see that? Didn't she have a tour to worry about? Why was she making this her problem? This was what police officers were for! He humbly told the valet they were really ready this time, and then hurried back to Maggie. They were both standing now. This time, he didn't hang back, but went right up to her. "Maggie, it's the middle of the night. The restaurants are all going to be closed."

Michael's face fell, and for that, Dane felt bad, but reality was reality.

"Stop it!" Maggie hissed through closed teeth. Then she looked down at Michael. "Don't worry. It might be hard, but we'll find her."

He looked comforted, but only a little.

"All right, let's go," Dane said, gesturing toward the entrance where the truck would soon be. He did *not* want to go along with this lunacy, but what else could he do? She was his boss. And besides, if he didn't go along with it, she would still do it, he was sure of it. So she'd be driving some strange kid all over Nashville with a hangover and a cast. Wait till the tabloids got hold of *that*.

He opened the back door of the SUV to allow his two new friends to climb in. Then he tipped the valet *again*. If Maggie didn't buy his breakfast, he wouldn't be eating. Then he climbed into the driver's seat.

"Do you know how to get to the airport?"

"Yes," he said through a clenched jaw. "I'm not an idiot."

He pulled the vehicle out onto the road. At least there wasn't much traffic.

"Turn the radio on," Maggie commanded from the back.

He didn't move.

"Did you hear me?"

"I did not hear the word 'please'—that's for sure."

He thought he heard her snicker, but he wasn't sure. "*Puh-lease* turn the radio on. We want to count the songs till we get to the airport."

Dane obliged this time, and the sound of Dan and Shay filled the space.

"You like this song?" Maggie said, and then she started snapping her fingers and singing along. He couldn't believe his ears. Maggie Hammer was all jagged rocks and sharp quills. He never would've guessed she had a soft side, let alone a side as soft as this.

# 23

Maggie could hardly keep her eyes open, despite the fact that her adrenaline was surging. Who leaves a kid in a hospital parking lot in the middle of the night? She hadn't come right out and asked him that, because she knew he wouldn't answer her if she did. At least, she wouldn't have answered some strange adult asking that question when she was his age. And while she'd never spent the night on a stone bench outside a hospital, she *had* run away from home more times than she could accurately count now, and she was certain she'd encountered the occasional probing adult during those adventures.

"Let me know if you see it," she said for the third time.

Michael stared out the window, his little eyes flicking from side to side as he scanned the landscape for something that looked familiar. Dane, she was grateful, was quiet. She knew that he wasn't entirely on board with this mission, but she didn't really care. He worked for *her*. And you just don't leave a child in distress.

"Pancakes," Michael blurted out after several minutes of silence.

"Pancakes?" she repeated cautiously. "She works at a place that serves pancakes?"

He nodded at her. "I think so."

*He thinks so. Awesome.* "Dane, I'm going to search for the closest pancake house. Hang on."

He didn't say anything.

She turned up the volume on her phone and laid it on the console between the two front bucket seats. It directed him, via the sultry voice of an Australian AI, toward the nearest flapjacks. He didn't comment on her choice of GPS narrator.

As he pulled into the parking lot of Pancake Castle, she asked, "Can you go in and ask if an Alice works here?"

He looked at her in the rearview. His face was impassive, yet she could still sense some low-level irritation beneath his placidity.

"I'd do it, but I'm much slower," she explained.

Wordlessly, Dane slid out of the truck and walked toward the restaurant. Maggie caught herself watching the back of his pants as he went. He looked better in jeans, but he was no slouch in dress pants either. She looked around the parking lot, which was almost empty.

"What if she's not here?" Michael asked quietly.

"Then we go to the next pancake place." She smiled at him in the dim light. "And if she's not there, we go to the next and the next and the next, until we've searched every pancake restaurant in Tennessee."

He giggled.

She reached over and rubbed his knee. "Don't worry, Michael. We'll find her."

The overhead light came on, momentarily blinding her, as Dane climbed back into the vehicle. "No dice," he said.

"Did you ask for her by last name?"

"Yes," he said, sounding defensive. "I know how to find out if someone works somewhere. They've never heard of her. They did, however, tell me about another pancake place on the other side of the airport."

"Awesome. Let's go."

Dane silently circled the giant property, and Maggie continued the battle of keeping her eyes open. But then as they pulled into the new lot, Michael started to bounce in his seat. "This is it! This is it!"

"Are you sure?" Maggie asked and then regretted it. It was obvious that he was sure. So, this time, after asking Dane to hand her a shoe, Maggie followed Dane into the restaurant, and Michael followed her. Dane still led the investigation, and Maggie didn't mind.

"Does someone named Alice work here?" he asked a middle-aged woman in a maroon apron. Her name tag read Sally Jo. "It's an emergency."

Sally Jo looked Dane up and down and then her eyes drifted to Michael and Maggie. She startled when her eyes rested on Maggie's face. Maggie hoped she hadn't placed her, but she didn't know if this hope would be realized. Whether Sally Jo recognized Maggie, she didn't say anything, and her eyes moved back to Dane's. Maggie couldn't blame her. He was the best-looking one in the bunch. "We're not supposed to give out personal information about employees," she said slowly. "But if you want to have a seat"—she pointed her chin toward a maroon, pleather bench that ran along the wall—"I've got to make a phone call. Then maybe we could talk after that."

"Great, thank you—" Dane started, but Maggie interrupted.

"Actually, we'd like to grab some food either way. Mind if we take a booth?"

She swept her arm toward the empty dining area. "Take your pick. I'll be right back."

Maggie grabbed some menus out of a wooden rack on the wall and handed them to Dane. Then she hobbled toward the closest booth. She felt light-headed, but she didn't know if that was a symptom of ankle sprain, hunger, or excessive champagne consumption. It was likely some combination of the three. Whatever was causing her vertigo, even though she'd only been on her feet, or on *one* foot rather, for about five minutes, she was still relieved to slide into the lumpy booth.

Dane passed out the menus, and with a long exhale, she flipped hers open, even though she didn't really need to look at the offerings. If she was going to splurge on pancakes, she was getting chocolate chip.

Sally Jo returned to their table. "What would you like to drink?"

What did that mean? Had she made the phone call or not?

Dane looked down at Michael. "What do you like to drink?"

"Water."

Dane looked at Sally Jo. "Three waters please, and I think we're ready to order too." He looked at Michael again. "Do you know what you want to eat?"

Michael turned his attention to the small notepad in Sally Jo's hand. "Chocolate chip Mickey Mouse pancakes, please. With whipped cream."

Sally Jo's face erupted into a giant smile as she made a note on her pad.

"I'll have the same," Maggie said, closing her menu and putting it on top of Michael's unopened one.

Dane snickered. "I'll just have the fruit cup, please."

"The fruit cup?" Maggie cried. "What, are you on a diet?" It occurred to her that he might not have any money. "I'm buying, you know. I always buy when I force my employees to search for strangers' grandmas."

One side of Dane's mouth curled up in something resembling a smile. He looked at Sally Jo. "*Two* fruit cups, please."

Sally nodded, jotted something down, and then vanished.

Dane turned his eyes back to Maggie, and she felt she might melt under their heat. "This job requires a certain level of physical fitness, you know."

"Oh, and mine doesn't?" Maggie cried, thinking about how much energy it took to zip back and forth across a stage while belting out ballads night after night.

"I said nothing of the sort. But I can't protect you if I'm in a sugar coma."

Oops. Of course he hadn't meant to suggest her job wasn't physical. Why was she always so easily offended?

"Protect?" Michael said, his eyes wide. "Are you her bodyguard or something?"

"That's right, little man. I would give my life for this woman."

# 24

Dane fought to be patient. How long did it take to put some canned fruit into a cup? Granted, his boss and her new little friend had ordered pancakes, but those didn't take a half hour to make. Michael colored on his placemat, Maggie fiddled with the salt and pepper shakers, and Dane literally twiddled his thumbs as the minutes ticked by. No other patrons came in, and Sally Jo was about as scarce as a server could be.

When the front door opened, Dane nearly leapt with excitement. Someone else to look at! The woman stepped inside, looked around the big room, and then made a beeline for them, and Dane knew this was Alice. He tapped Michael on the arm and then pointed to the approaching woman.

"Grammy!" Michael cried. He jumped out of his seat and ran to her.

Dane got up and slid into the opposite seat, to make room for Alice and her grandson to sit together. Maggie looked at him with what looked like surprise in her eyes and he hoped he wasn't being too assuming by sitting beside her. His arm brushed against hers as he settled in, and the little hairs on his arm stood at attention with visible goosebumps beneath them. Embarrassed, he hurried to rub his arm. "Cold in here," he said.

"Uh-huh," Maggie said, not sounding convinced.

Michael returned, holding Alice's hand in his. "This is Maggie." He pointed to her.

"Maggie," Alice said, with tears in her eyes, "I can't thank you enough. What happened? I don't understand."

Dane gestured toward the empty side of the booth. "You're welcome to have a seat, if you want. Michael has some Mickey Mouse pancakes coming, if you'd like to stick around for a few minutes."

"Sure!" She sat down, and Michael scooted in beside her.

"I don't really know what happened," Maggie started, and then *finally*, Sally Jo appeared and slid plates in front of them.

"Do you want anything to eat?" Sally Jo asked Alice.

"Just some coffee, please."

"You bet. Cream?"

"No thank you. Black as midnight, please."

"Coming right up."

Dane took a bite of his fruit cup. It was terrible. He was really going to have to work to eat two servings of canned pears and maraschino cherries. But he'd eaten grosser things. It was hard to beat the "jambalaya with shrimp" MRE on the grossness scale.

Maggie started to cut into her pancakes. "These are cold!" she cried, sounding unreasonably angry. If she got that upset about cold pancakes, Dane was glad she'd never had to endure the bagged jambalaya.

"I think Sally Jo was stalling," Dane said, "afraid we would leave before Alice got here."

Maggie didn't look comforted by this idea and dropped her silverware with a loud clank. "So, I don't know what happened. You'll have to ask Michael. I found him sitting alone outside the hospital. He told me about you, and that you worked at a pancake restaurant, so we came here. That's it."

*She makes it sound so simple*, Dane thought. But he certainly wasn't going to correct her.

Alice looked down at Michael, who had already eaten both of Mickey Mouse's ears. "What happened, honey? Where's Mom?"

He shrugged, looking embarrassed.

"You don't have to tell her in front of us," Maggie said, and Dane was impressed with her intuitive empathy. Maggie opened her purse and pulled out some cash, which she tossed toward the center of the table. She nudged Dane, who had just grudgingly started on his second fruit cup. "Come on, get me home. Let's let them get on with their night."

"Wait!" Alice said. "You're Maggie Hammer, aren't you?"

Maggie offered her a tired smile and nodded. "Guilty."

"You're nothing like I expected." She paused, and then hurried to add, "I mean that as a compliment. Not that I was expecting anything bad."

Maggie chuckled. "I understand. And yeah, don't believe everything you read in the tabloids." She reached across the table and squeezed Michael's hand. "Bye, Michael. It was nice to meet you." Then she was sliding her body into Dane's again. He considered not moving, so that she'd keep pressing her body against his, but this would be fairly obnoxious, so he slid out of the seat.

"I don't know how to thank you," Alice said.

"No need. He was a kid alone in the dark. Anyone would've done it." She smiled and then turned and slowly made her way toward the door, swinging on her crutches with an awkwardness that made it clear she'd never had to use crutches before.

# 25

Maggie pulled herself into the front of the SUV, and Dane shut the door behind her. It was getting chilly out. She reached down and turned up the heat knob, even though the vehicle wasn't even running yet.

Dane climbed in and started the engine. Then he looked at her.

"What?" His stare made her self-conscious.

"Isn't it going to drive you crazy? The not knowing?"

She shrugged. "None of my business."

"I know. I'm just nosy, I guess."

Maggie knew how important secrets could be, and how awful it felt when strangers learned those secrets. "I can think up a handful of scenarios. One of them is probably correct. That's enough. The mom was scared, so she dropped him off somewhere she thought was safe, probably told him to go inside. Or mom is an addict. Or she's skipping town, and she told someone else to pick him up, and they didn't. It doesn't matter which sad story it is. They're all the same, really. Parents not doing their job."

He was quiet for several moments, and she was almost asleep when he said, "You're wrong, you know."

Her chest tightened with defensiveness. "Wrong about what?"

"Most people would *not* have done that. In fact, I don't know anyone who would have done what you just did. Why didn't you just call the police?"

Maggie made a derisive *pfft* sound. Yeah, right. The police. "Let's just say I didn't have great experiences with police when *I* was the kid in trouble."

"Well ..." he sounded hesitant.

"What? Spit it out."

"You can't hold *all* police accountable for the way a couple of them behaved when you were a kid."

"Whatever. Just drive." She wasn't going to argue with her bodyguard.

"Sorry. I just meant to say that I was impressed, and the way you were with him ... it was just ..." He hesitated, and she held her breath to make sure she didn't miss whatever he was going to say next. "It was just admirable. It was sweet. Compassionate. Special."

Her cheeks were on fire, and that warmth was spreading down through the rest of her. She got praised all the time; why was praise from this guy having such a profound effect on her? "Thanks," she said, sounding unsure.

"You're welcome. You obviously have a giant heart. That's what I'm trying to say. And this image you're projecting to the world, well, *that's* not it."

"What's that supposed to mean?" she snapped.

He was quiet for an obnoxiously long time. "I'm not trying to insult you. I just wish your fans, or the people you're trying to get to be your fans, well, I wish they knew the real you."

"They do. Tonight was only one part of the real me. There's more to me than being nice to a lost kid."

"I know that. But ..." His voice trailed off.

"What?" she tried to prod him.

"Never mind."

"No, tell me."

He took a deep breath and twisted his hands on the steering wheel with so much pressure that they squeaked. "Promise not to fire me?"

Her giggle surprised her. She didn't think she had enough energy to giggle. "Of course not."

"Okay, well, this public persona of yours is not that of a nice person, of a kind person, even of a good person. What you did tonight makes you an absolute sweetheart. Sometimes, you're not a sweetheart. Sometimes, you're a little sour."

Wow. He shot straight from the hip. She didn't know how to respond. But she wasn't offended. Because he was absolutely right. "It's different with kids."

"How?"

"Because kids are kids. They're innocent. Adults are jerks, and they should know better."

He turned to face her in the darkness, but she didn't look at him. "I'm not sure that makes any sense."

"That's okay." She looked out the window. "It makes sense to me." How could she explain to him that she was almost always angry about something, almost always afraid of something? Always fighting for something.

They were quiet for the rest of the ride home, and Maggie fought to keep her eyes open. She was afraid that if she fell asleep in the truck, she wouldn't be able to fall asleep when she finally made it into her bed, and she was desperate to sleep through this pain.

Dane turned the engine off. "Do you need help getting inside?"

"I'm not an invalid," she snapped, even though she felt like one. She gingerly slid to the pavement, and by the time she got there, Dane had her crutches ready for her. "Thank you."

"You're welcome." He scanned the area and then motioned toward the door, shutting and locking her truck behind her. She started toward the door, but he got ahead of her with key in hand. Suddenly, his closed fist flew into the air. She didn't know what the motion meant, but it had an ominous feel to it.

"What?"

He moved the hand to the front of her, not actually touching her, but making sure she didn't move any further ahead, like a mom who slams on the brakes and then checks to make sure her child's seatbelt worked.

"What?" she said again.

He slid a phone out of his pocket and held it up like he was going to take a picture of her front door. And then she saw it. A piece of paper taped to her door. She reached to grab it, and he stopped her by grabbing her hand. At his touch, her body exploded in electricity, which annoyed her immensely. She didn't have time for bodyguard sparks. Not ever, but especially not now. "Let me have it!"

"No. We're calling the police."

"We are not calling anyone!" She stepped closer to see what the note said.

In that now familiar looping handwriting, the note said, "It's not too late to make this right. You don't want to suffer the consequences." Her stomach rolled over. What kind of a psycho was this guy?

"Get back into the truck."

"No! I want to go to bed!" She'd never been so desperate for a pillow in her life.

"It's not safe. The guy's been here."

"How?" Maggie cried. She looked toward the gate they'd just driven through. "Security wouldn't have let anyone in."

"He came on foot. It's not hard to climb a fence."

The idea of that gave her the shivers. Someone went to all that trouble just to tape a note to her door?

Dane snapped a few photos and then took her by the arm. "Let's get back into the truck. You can sleep in there."

"I need my pillow!"

"You *need* to be safe. Now get in the truck." He didn't raise his voice, but his tone made it clear that he wasn't making a request. Normally, she didn't like being bossed around by *anyone*, but something about the way he did it made it okay. She still didn't want to sleep in the truck, but she would do what he said to do. She didn't know why, but she trusted him.

# 26

By the time Dane finished talking to the police, the sun was high and bright in the sky. It didn't seem to be bothering Maggie though, who was stretched out in the backseat, snoring soundly. A police officer had woken her up to ask her a few questions, and Maggie had been considerably less than cordial, so the interview hadn't lasted long. The police had swept the condo, determined there was no danger, and, as Maggie had predicted, didn't seem overly concerned about her safety. Maybe this sort of thing happened to country stars all the time. He had no idea. He also didn't care. Even if this stuff came with the territory and didn't mean anything, he would act like there was a serious threat. Her life might depend on it. He would rather overreact than lose her.

He carried her into her bedroom and carefully laid her on her mattress. She only stirred a little in his arms, and he felt bad for her. Her being in physical pain made his stomach roll, and he wished he could take the pain from her. He took off her shoe, and then pulled a blanket up to her chin before leaving the room. Then, even though he trusted the police had done a thorough search of the place, he went over every inch again, just to make sure.

Finally satisfied that there was nothing to find, he collapsed onto his own bed and was asleep in seconds. He dreamed of Sherman, his brother, his friend. He dreamed of fire, of trying to pull Sherman out of the fire, of Sherman hollering at him to go, to leave him there, but he wouldn't. He couldn't. In the dream, he knew he was going to die, but then he felt strong arms pulling on him, dragging him away from Sherman and toward safety. He screamed, "No!" at the top of his lungs, but his voice got lost in the roar of the fire. Then he saw that they were pulling Sherman out too, and then he knew—they were both going to live.

Except that they didn't both live. Dane barely made it out alive, and Sherman didn't. He was gone. "No!" Dane cried as he stared at his lifeless friend, willing his chest to rise, begging the universe to rewind, to change its mind. "No!"

Someone was shaking his leg. He sat bolt upright, his heart pounding, and looked around the small room. Where was he?

Then his life rushed in like a cool wave, washing away the dream, trying to wash away the past, and he was returned to the present. Maggie sat on the edge of his bed, concern etched across her brow. Her small, perfectly manicured hand rested on his thigh.

"Are you okay?" Her voice sounded raspy.

He ran a hand through his hair. "Just a bad dream. Sorry. Was I talking?"

She hesitated. "You were *screaming*."

"Sorry," he said again. He was embarrassed. Why couldn't he control himself when he dreamed? It was so frustrating.

She rubbed his leg. "No, don't be sorry. First of all, you don't have to apologize for having bad dreams. You can't control that."

She hit that nail on the head. Maybe she had some experience with bad dreams herself.

"*And* you were a soldier. I can't even imagine seeing the things you saw, experiencing the things you went through, and you did it all to protect our country, our freedom, our way of life. Dane, you're a hero."

He flinched. He didn't like being called a hero. He hadn't been able to save Sherman. He hadn't saved anyone. He nodded to pacify her. "Thanks. What time is it?" He tried to collect his thoughts.

She removed her hand, which left his leg feeling lonely, and took a big breath. "It's time to go, I'm afraid. The label has called. They're not happy."

Of course they weren't. "And they want to meet with you?"

"Yep. Like five minutes ago. So, sorry to rush you, but ..."

He could take a hint. "Yeah, just give me five."

He was out the door in two. She was already waiting by the truck. "I wish you wouldn't do that."

"What, go outside without you?" She said it as if that was a foolish thing to wish.

"Yes. You could've waited inside."

"I could've," she said flippantly, and opened her own door to climb into the front seat.

He shook his head and walked around the vehicle, scanning their surroundings for anything amiss, but all was quiet and still.

"I know you're afraid of this guy, Maggie, so why don't you just take simple precautions?"

"Because I know he's not going to grab me in broad daylight between my house and the truck." She flipped her hair over her shoulder, and the gesture was both obnoxious and alluring.

Traffic slowed them down a little, but they made it to Sequin headquarters in fifteen minutes. Maggie was wringing her hands and bouncing her knee up and down.

"Nervous?"

"No." She didn't sound half-convincing.

He wanted to comfort her, but he had no idea what was going to happen. He helped her out of the SUV and waited for her to get her crutches under her. Then he walked alongside her, slowly, as they made their way to the doors.

The air conditioning assaulted them as soon as they stepped inside. A receptionist offered a fake smile and said, "I'll let them know you're here." Dane waited for Maggie to sit down on one of the sofas or chairs in the waiting area, but she stood firm.

It wasn't a long wait. A short, stocky man with big glasses came through a door. "Hi, Maggie." He looked at Dane. "Who's this?"

"My bodyguard."

"Oh, okay." The man stuck out his hand. "I'm Albert Erlebach, Maggie's publicist. You won't mind waiting out here, will you? I'll have Danielle get you some coffee—"

"He goes with me."

Albert gave her a long look, and Dane wondered if he was debating whether to argue with her. Evidently, he decided against it, because he looked at Dane and said, "Right this way."

Dane followed the two of them down a narrow hallway. Albert got quite a lead on them as Maggie wasn't moving too quickly, so when he reached his destination, he had to stop and wait for them to catch up.

Dane was the last one to step into the large conference room, and the tension was thick. Several important-looking people sat around a giant table that looked like mahogany, and it appeared they had all just dined on something sour. Dane took his spot beside the open door, trying to be invisible. He said a silent prayer for Maggie. This didn't look good.

"Maggie," one of the men said, "we're canceling the tour."

To her credit, Maggie didn't freak out. She just sat there looking at him, with fire in her eyes.

"I'm sure you can understand. You can't perform on crutches."

"Yes, I can."

He snickered. "Don't be ridiculous. Your current single is 'Wild Child.' You can't be a wild child on crutches. Even *if* the single wasn't already falling off the charts."

Dane could tell that Maggie felt that verbal slap, but she came right back with, "I'll wear a floor-length gown. I come out on stage in the dark. The lights go up, and I act like I'm not in pain." The man who was apparently in charge opened his mouth to argue with her, but she didn't give him a chance. "I'll faithfully do my physical therapy on the road. I'll take good care of myself and heal as quickly as possible. It won't be a problem."

He looked speechless.

"You got drunk and fell off a stage!" a man in an orange shirt said. "So you telling us that you're going to take care of yourself isn't exactly reassuring."

Maggie turned her fiery eyes on him. "You don't want to cancel this tour. If you do, Blayze Balin will find a different tour."

Mr. Orange Shirt snorted. "So? What do we care about Blayze Balin?"

Maggie leaned toward the table and spoke slowly, "You care because he and I are dating, and the fans *love us together*. Splitting us up will ruin a great opportunity."

She was lying through her teeth. Wasn't she? Why was she doing this?

The original speaker said, "I couldn't care less about you helping Blayze's image—"

"It's not about his image," Maggie spat, "it's about the fact that fans *love* him, and them loving him makes them love me, and he and I are putting a duet on my album."

"What duet?" a woman on the other side of the table snapped. "I didn't okay any duet."

Maggie cocked her head to one side and looked at the woman, who was so obviously not a fan. "You don't have to *okay* anything. My contract says I have to deliver commercially viable songs, and that's what I'll do." She returned her gaze to the head honcho. "When you signed me, you bet on me. Don't lose that investment. I can do this."

He lowered his voice. "You fired your manager. Not only does that show incredibly bad judgment, but it also means you have no one to manage you—"

"I didn't *fire* him. He quit. And I don't need a manager."

Mr. Head Honcho tipped his head back and laughed. "Oh yeah? Why's that?"

"Because she has me," a man said as he stepped into the room. He wore a suit and a perfect haircut, and Dane moved to block his path, but he stuck his hand out toward Dane. "Hello, Dane, my name is Oliver Vogl. Aunt Sally Jo sends her regards."

# 27

Maggie forced her jaw closed. She knew the name Oliver Vogl. He was young and hadn't been managing very long, but he'd managed two different acts from obscurity to stardom, where they'd promptly dumped him, upgrading him for people with more experience and better connections. Maggie would *never* do that to him. She couldn't believe he was here, and she had every confidence in his abilities.

"May I?" he said, pointing to the empty chair beside her.

John, the Marketing Coordinator who was currently acting as though he was running the show, nodded.

Oliver unbuttoned his suit jacket and sat. "Maggie is injured, but she can do the tour. I'll personally oversee it and make sure she doesn't further injure herself, while giving the ticket buyers their money's worth. More importantly, Maggie's image is injured, and I will repair that too."

John didn't look convinced. "You seem to have a high opinion of your abilities."

"When does the album drop?" Oliver asked.

"As soon as she gets the songs cut."

Oliver looked at her. "How many more songs do you have to record?"

"One."

"When can you do it?"

"Right now."

Oliver looked at John. "Can someone get her some studio time? The faster this album gets out, the faster you make your money, and the happier you are. I'll take care of the rest. We'll get her on radio.

We'll get magazines, podcasts, and television. Just give her a chance." He flashed her a grin. "Give *us* a chance."

They pounded out the details, and before Maggie knew it, she really was headed out on tour on crutches. Now that it was really going to happen, the idea concerned her a little. Maybe she could ride a scooter around the stage? She zoned out as they wrapped up the meeting. She couldn't believe how well this was all panning out for her. She'd made a royal mess of things the night before, but then the perfect manager had fallen out of the sky into her lap. She really needed to get back to the pancake house and thank Sally Jo.

Oliver looked at her. "Let's go get a drink."

She smiled and nodded, only grimacing a little at the pain that shot up her leg when she stood. He reached out to steady her, and she saw Dane step toward them, as if Oliver posed some sort of threat or he just didn't like Oliver touching her. She followed Oliver out into the hallway and then toward the door, with Dane trailing behind.

Once they got outside, she said to Oliver, "I think I should lay off the alcohol for a while, but I could go for a root beer."

Oliver grinned broadly. "Sure, let's go for a round of root beers. On me. How about Mavericks?"

"Sure."

"Great. Mind if I hitch a ride with y'all?"

She shook her head. "Of course not." She looked at Dane. "Is that all right with you?" Then she wondered why she'd asked him that. He was just the bodyguard; he really shouldn't get a vote.

Dane nodded, and the newly formed threesome headed toward the Ford.

When they reached it, Maggie turned to look at Oliver. "I get that Sally Jo wanted to thank me for helping her friend, but you're going above and beyond. Thank you." She felt as though she wanted to say more, as though she *should* say more, to convey her gratitude, but the words just weren't coming.

Oliver looked at her with gravity in his eyes. "Maggie, Sally Jo didn't ask me to help you. She just told me how she'd met you ... *and* how she'd overheard you talking about how your manager had quit. Anyway, I'm here because I'm a fan, and because I think you've gotten a bad rap for leaving your family. I think that was a smart move. You're light years ahead of them, and they were holding you back. You're going to be huge, Maggie Hammer, and I'd like to be there when that happens." He held up his left hand and wiggled his ring finger. "And I'm a happily married newlywed, so you can be sure my intentions are pure."

She didn't know what to say, so she said nothing. Dane opened the front door for her, and she climbed in. "Congratulations," he whispered into her ear, and she was so happy she had to fight back the tears.

# 28

D ane was dreaming again. It was almost always the same dream. He'd tried everything to make the nightmares stop: praying, asking for prayer from others, medications, herbs, journaling. He'd tried counseling and "making the dream have a good ending" by visualizing the dream before falling asleep. But nothing worked. Not yet anyway. The heat from the fire's flames made the sweat pour out of him. It was too hot to breathe, too hot to think, and then he was being pulled, pulled away from Sherman, and he was screaming at whoever was pulling him—screaming at them to stop. He waved his arms at them, trying to stop them from pulling him, and he felt his hot skin collide with cool, soft skin that didn't belong.

"Stop it!" a female voice screeched at him. He knew that voice didn't belong, but he didn't understand where it was coming from, and he flailed his arms even harder in his confusion. The cool hands pushed harder on his arms. "Stop it! You're hitting me!" And then there were cool, soft lips on his, and he froze. This didn't make sense. Who was kissing him? Who was pushing his arms to the ground—except that it wasn't the ground, it was a bed, and he knew where he was and whose cool hands were on his hot skin. Maggie Hammer was kissing him.

He pulled away. "Sorry," he mumbled, as the embarrassment washed over him for the thousandth time. Maybe he couldn't be a bodyguard. Maybe he couldn't have a job that had him anywhere near someone else at night. He pinched the bridge of his nose and tried to slow his breathing. But what other job could he do? If he was going to use his skill set, then this was it. Or he could look for a daily security gig, maybe at a bank or something. Yes, maybe that made more sense.

He was afraid to open his eyes, afraid to look at her. Why had she just kissed him?

"What did I tell you about apologizing for things you can't control?"

He opened one eye.

She had a hand over her mouth, as if she couldn't believe what she'd just done, as if she hadn't meant to do it.

"Did you just kiss me?"

She looked down at her hands. "I think so. Sorry. I didn't know what else to do. I was trying to snap you out of whatever that was."

"It was a nightmare," he said, but he wasn't sure if he'd said it out loud or just thought it. He was still a little groggy.

"Obviously. Scoot over." She pushed on his hip, and he rolled onto his side to make room for her. She lay down beside him and propped her head on her hand, gingerly laying her casted foot atop her good foot.

"Do you want a pillow for that?"

"Sure."

He grabbed one of his pillows from the head of the bed and then slowly lifted her foot so he could slide the pillow beneath it.

"Thanks."

"You're welcome," he said, and then returned to his spot, acutely aware that lying down beside his boss was not a good idea. "You can go now. I'm okay. I'm sor—" He caught himself and stopped talking.

"I'll go in a minute. I'm not trying to seduce you or anything." She giggled, but it came out staccato, nothing like the lilting cadence she shared when she was genuinely amused. "Tell me about your dream."

*Oh no.* "I'd rather not." He expected her to insist, to nag it out of him, to demand he obey her order.

But she didn't. She ran her hand down his arm and it made his whole body break out in goosebumps. "Of course you don't want to. I wouldn't want to either. But it might help. It's helped me in the past. I used to have bad dreams."

He forced himself to laugh. "I can't believe you kissed me." He was trying to distract her. He wished he could remember more about that kiss.

"Well, don't let it go to your head. I was just trying to yank you out of the dream. Now, tell me about it." Her eyes were so sincere that he felt persuaded. Was he really going to do this? Was he really going to talk to Maggie Hammer about his past trauma?

His lips started moving of their own accord. Yes, apparently, he was really going to do this. "My friend Sherman. He died overseas. I was there. I tried to save him. I couldn't."

She waited for him to say more. He let her wait. "It wasn't your fault," she whispered.

"I know," he said. "But it still sucks. I wish it had been me."

She wrapped her arm around him and nuzzled into his chest. "I can understand that," she mumbled, and he could feel the warmth of her breath through his T-shirt, "but I'm sure glad it wasn't you."

# 29

Maggie woke up nestled into Dane's side and instantly flew into a panic. She sat up so quickly that she moved her bad ankle and pain shot up her leg. She almost cried out but managed to stop herself. She bit her lip so hard that the pain almost rivaled the ankle pain. She didn't want to wake Dane up.

But that was easier said than done. The man was a light sleeper, and it was really hard to tiptoe out of a bedroom on crutches.

"You okay?" he called after her.

"Fine," she said without turning around. "Just need the bathroom."

She did go the bathroom and then used the mirror to give herself a good stare down. She did *not* have feelings for her bodyguard, did she? Oh shoot, she probably did. Who wouldn't? He was gorgeous, heroic, kind, and thoughtful. Shoot. She should not be having feelings. For anyone. Ever.

Because Maggie Hammer didn't even believe in love. Sure, she sang songs about it, but in reality, she thought it was for the birds. And even if she did change her mind—and that was a big "if"—she didn't need to be involved with the *bodyguard*. That would do *nothing* for her career, and her career was what mattered right now. If she was going to get involved with someone, it needed to be someone like Blayze. She took a deep breath and then, with great resolve, turned to leave the bathroom and face Dane.

Sure enough, she found him in the kitchen making fresh squeezed orange juice. Her mouth began to water. *Because of the juice*, she told herself, *not the man making it*. She swallowed hard.

"Want some?" he asked without looking at her.

"Sure, thanks. And I just want to put a few things out into the open."

He held up one hand. "You don't have to say it. I get it."

"You do?" What did he get, exactly?

He looked at her, and his expression looked content, peaceful, so different from last night, when the light spilling into his room from the hallway had shown a face contorted with horror. "Yeah. I get it. Nothing will ever happen between us. You're the boss. I'm the bodyguard." He turned his attention back to the oranges. "And that's fine. Thanks for doing what you had to do to wake me up. I appreciate it."

"You're welcome," she stammered. He'd given *her* the speech! She was supposed to give *him* the speech! She wasn't sure how she felt about this. Was he not interested in her? He'd certainly seemed that way last night. Not that he'd done anything to clearly indicate interest, but she'd gotten that vibe. The way he'd held her. The way he'd let her hold him. She hadn't meant to fall asleep there.

He smiled and slid her a glass of fresh juice.

She was desperate to say something, anything, to indicate that she was the one in control of this scenario. "And I wanted to tell you," she said, without being sure what she was going to tell him. But then it came to her. "I'm getting two tour buses."

His eyes widened. It was clear he knew what she meant. "You don't have to do that."

She took a swig of the juice, and it tasted like heaven. She drained the glass and then wiped her mouth self-consciously. "No, it's okay. I want to. I want you to be comfortable, but mostly, I just want my space. It's more about me than about you."

He didn't look convinced. "Well, then, thank you. And if you change your mind, that'll be okay too. I don't need to sleep much."

She stared at him. She had other questions she wanted to ask him, but she didn't want to pry. "Is it always the same nightmare?"

He nodded. "Pretty much." He slid onto a stool and rubbed his eyes.

She headed toward the coffee pot, keeping her back to him. "And how often do you have it?"

He didn't answer at first, and she forced herself not to look at him. If he didn't want to answer, he didn't have to. Then he did. "Pretty often. Sometimes I'll go for days without it, and I'll think I've got it licked, but then it will come back with a vengeance."

With the coffee brewing, she turned to look at him, leaning back on the counter. "Well, let me know if there's anything I can do. I've got your back."

He grinned broadly. "I thought I was supposed to have your back."

She nodded. "That too. I think we make a good team."

# 30

Dane stood in the darkness as two stagehands followed Maggie to center stage so that they could carry the crutches back. Dane wasn't sure why that was a two-man job, but he was happy to not be in charge of crutch-retrieval. Had it been a stadium show, and had Maggie been a bit more financially fit, she probably could have arrived via a smoke-ensconced lift. But this was a small theater, and that wasn't happening yet. And by the time Maggie could afford it, she wouldn't physically need it anymore. Thinking about her financial state made him feel guilty that she was paying for an extra tour bus. She told him she wasn't doing it for him, but he didn't believe her.

Maggie let out the long first note of "Popcorn Love," a song he thought he'd grow tired of fairly quickly. Maggie had alluded to the fact that it wasn't her favorite either. But the crowd loved it. They came to life at the sound of her gutsy alto, and then the lights came up, bathing her multitudinous sequins and instantly transforming her into a disco ball. *That's not quite accurate*, he thought. She was far more beautiful than a disco ball. She sang the entire song, which was as upbeat as its name suggested, firmly rooted to center stage, hanging onto the microphone stand. She was gripping it so firmly, he was worried that she was using it for support. She twitched her hip a little, but other than that, she stood still.

When she finished the song, she said, "Hi, Atlanta. My name is Maggie Hammer."

The crowd cheered, sounding bigger than it was.

"Thanks so much for the love. You have no idea how much I appreciate it."

*She sounds so sincere,* Dane thought, and wondered why that surprised him so much. He scanned the audience, looking for anything suspicious, but his eyes soon drifted back to center stage. He was supposed to be watching everyone *but* Maggie. That was proving to be harder than it should be.

"You know, I'm going to sing a song called 'Wild Child' in a bit." She paused to allow for the crowd to cheer their appreciation of this. "And it's true, you may have heard, I can be a bit of a wild child." She paused for laughter. She certainly knew how to work a crowd. Dane couldn't see her face, but he could hear the smile in her voice. And the voice she was using now was nothing like the one she used in real life. She was performing, and she sounded more comfortable performing than she did speaking to him in her own living room. *How strange.*

"Sometimes, being a wild child has its perks." She tipped her head back and to the side, laughing at her own words, but she quickly returned to the mic. "And sometimes it doesn't." Slowly, she reached down and pinched part of her gown and slid it up her leg. Maggie Hammer could even make exposing a cast look sexy. Dane shook his head in wonder. A few oohs and aahs sounded from the crowd, but for the most part, they were quiet, hanging on her every word. "Some people wanted me to cancel the show ..." She stopped to allow for the boos. "But I wouldn't do that to y'all. So, I'm not going to be dancing tonight, and sorry, no crowd surfing. That's what got me into this mess." *Well,* that *was a small exaggeration.* "But I brought some extra dancers with me, and they dance better than I do, *and* I'm going to do a few extra songs for you, just to make sure you get your money's worth." The crowd cheered its appreciation of this promise. "And for one of those songs, we'll bring Blayze back out on stage." They loved that too. This crowd was easy to please. Without further ado, the band started another upbeat number, "Back Road Sunshine," and two professional dancers front-flipped their way onto the stage until they flanked

Maggie. Dane hadn't been expecting them. *They must live on the other bus.*

They danced for three songs in a row, and they were amazing to watch. Then they slipped offstage as one black-clad crew member slid a stool under Maggie, while another slid her mandolin strap over her neck.

"Let's bring it down for a second and get real," Maggie said. "That okay with y'all?" Of course it was. She began to pick the intro to "Long Hard Road," and a lump formed in Dane's throat. That song may have been made for Nitty Gritty Dirt Band, but it was also made for Maggie Hammer. The fans agreed with him, and these *were* undoubtably, *fans.* Not just country music lovers, not just concert goers. He could tell by the enthusiasm of their applause and cheers. They *loved* Maggie Hammer. He was relieved to hear it. She *did* have support. Not a stadium's worth, but this theater crowd was nothing to sneeze at. Blayze appeared beside him, his electric slung over his shoulder. He didn't even grant Dane a glance, which was fine with him.

Maggie finished "Long Hard Road" and then called Blayze out on stage. Then, to Dane's horror, she planted her lips on his when he got there. Dane thought he was going to be sick. He hadn't realized this charade was still on. As far as he knew, she hadn't so much as spoken to the guy while they'd been on the road. Dane was suddenly *very* grateful that Blayze had his own bus. They started to sing their song, and Blayze was standing awfully close to Maggie. She rubbed her bottom up against him, and Dane had to fight not to march out onto the stage and pull them apart.

Oliver materialized beside him. "Aren't they something?" he said, his voice loaded with admiration.

Dane felt sick. "They're something all right."

Oliver looked at him quickly, studied his face for a moment, making Dane self-conscious, and then returned his eyes to the dynamic duo. "Jealous?"

"Not at all," Dane said quickly. Too quickly. "I just don't trust him," he added, trying to sound more rational, less emotional. "And I'm not sure he's as good for her image as she thinks he is." He forced himself to stop talking. Why was he still talking?

Oliver looked at him again. "He is *great* for her image. She wants to be seen as desirable, right? So, let's tell the world that the most desirable country bachelor *desires her.*"

Dane wished he hadn't said anything.

"And, it doubles her exposure. He's got a lot of eyeballs on him. We want all those eyes on her too." He gave Dane's upper arm a friendly sock. "Don't we, now?"

Dane realized that he wasn't sure if he wanted that. Of course, he wanted Maggie to be successful, but at what cost? Couldn't she just be herself, and let *that* make her successful? But he didn't say any of that to Oliver. He'd said enough for one night.

# 31

Maggie tried to be patient as she and Blayze waited at the bar for a table. What kind of a podunk town doesn't let the visiting artists jump the line? She'd tried to insist, but they'd claimed all the tables were full, promising the next empty one available. Whatever. Now she was sitting at a bar full of suits, pretending to care about whatever Blayze was blathering on about. He was already on his second beer. She wondered what Dane was thinking and had to force herself not to look behind her. She knew he was there, watching, and didn't know why she had the almost overpowering urge to check.

"So, you happy with the way the tour's going?"

"Sure." He took a haul off his beer. "But we're only a few weeks in, aren't we?"

What did that mean? She decided to stop talking to him.

During Blayze's third beer, when she was considering abandoning this date altogether, a teenage girl shyly approached them. "Um, excuse me?"

Maggie turned to give the girl her best smile and her full attention.

"Are you"—she giggled nervously—"Blayze Balin?" She spoke his name as if the name itself provoked awe.

"Why, yes I am, sugar. And who do I have the pleasure of meeting?" He held out his hand.

Maggie finally gave in and glanced in Dane's direction, and found that he was only a few feet away, his face lined with concern. She waved him off. This girl was obviously no threat.

"I'm Patrice." She took his hand, and her whole body trembled.

Maggie almost failed to avoid her eye roll, but at the last second, she pulled herself together.

"I was wondering if I like, could have your autograph?"

"Of course you can! What would you like me to sign?"

*Good grief, could he be any louder?*

Patrice shrugged.

Blayze waved the bartender over and asked him for a pen, which he used to sign a napkin. "To Patrice, so nice to meet you. Blayze Balin." He handed it to her, and another bout of quivers overtook her.

"Thank you." She giggled and then scurried back into the crowd of people waiting for a table.

Blayze sat back down. "She was nice."

Maggie punched him in the side.

"Ow! What was that for?"

"You didn't even introduce me!"

He did *not* hold back his own eye roll. "Didn't realize I was your publicity person. Can't help it if *I'm* the famous one."

She hated him. "If you're so *famous*, why aren't you the headliner?"

He gave her a dirty look. "You know why."

She did know why. He was a troublemaker, and no one wanted him. Maybe she shouldn't have thrown that in his face. Nah, he deserved it.

The hostess appeared. "Your table is ready."

"About time," Maggie snapped. *This food had better be out of this world.* She grabbed her purse and followed the hostess to the table. She noticed Blayze staring at the hostess's bottom and thought about punching him again, but refrained. There were a lot of people there. She had to be on her best behavior. She glanced back to see that Dane was following them into the dining room, and as the hostess seated them, Dane faded into a dark corner. No one paid him any mind. He was good at being invisible.

A server appeared and asked what they wanted to drink. Blayze ordered another beer and then looked at Maggie. "You'll have a lot more fun if you have a drink."

Maggie smiled at the server. "I'll have a sweet tea, please."

"I meant a real drink."

"I know." She snapped her menu open and buried her face in it.

Her phone buzzed with a notification from Chattalot, an app she used so infrequently that it took her a second to even recognize the small icon that popped up. She figured it was spam and ignored it.

"What are you going to have?" Blayze asked.

She closed the menu. She wanted to order a chocolate cake. "I'm going to have the Southwestern Salad."

He snorted. "I thought Texan women ate steak."

Why did thousands of women find him endearing? Oh right, because they didn't know him.

"You need to loosen up a little," he said.

"What?" Heat crept up her neck.

"Why can't you just have a drink like a normal person? You know, live a little? And why do you have to check to make sure your bodyguard is in position every two seconds?"

"I am not checking—!" she started to protest but then realized how she sounded—a bit unhinged. She calmed herself down. "I'm not checking every two seconds."

"I still don't understand why he had to come. I'm perfectly capable of protecting my date."

"I'm sure you are," she said, even though she wasn't sure of any such thing. "But he takes his job seriously. And well ..." She didn't want to tell Blayze the details of her life, but she *did* want him to know why she had such an attentive bodyguard. She wanted him to know there was a professional reason for Dane's presence. "I've had some threats," she blurted out before she could further agonize over whether to tell Blayze about her stalker.

He raised an eyebrow, looking interested in something for the first time that evening. "Threats?"

Her phone buzzed again. She looked down to see that same icon. What, had her Chattalot app just sprang to life? She nodded at Blayze. "Yeah, some letters, and they're pretty creepy, so I hired Dane. He was a soldier, and he's tough as nails. Fearless." The server set her tea in front of her, and she took a long swallow.

Blayze looked over his shoulder at Dane. "Do you have the hots for him?"

"No!" she cried.

Blayze snickered. "Sure."

"Why would you say that?"

He shrugged. "I don't know. You won't let anyone else on your tour bus. Just you two holed up together all those long nights on the road."

"Don't be ridiculous." She couldn't tell him the *real* reason she didn't have anyone else sleeping on her bus. "It's a professional relationship."

"It might be, but you want it to be more."

She really wanted him to shut up. "Why don't you just drink your beer."

"You do. I can tell by the way your face lights up when you tell me how tough he is, and I can see it in your eyes when you look at him."

"So," she said, desperate to change the subject, "did you hear? 'Long Hard Road' is at number nine."

"Congratulations. They should've released our song first. I didn't spend all night in the studio recording so that it could sit as an album cut."

She gave him a crooked smile. "You could always have *your* label release it as a single."

"Oh yeah!" He laughed. "They nearly croaked when they found out I was recording with you. They're not your biggest fans."

She wasn't offended. She understood their position. From their point of view, it seemed she'd abandoned them, abandoned her contract with them. They didn't understand, didn't have any idea what her family was really like.

Her phone buzzed again.

"Who *is* that?" Blayze said and snatched up her phone.

She was only slightly irritated. There was nothing worth hiding on that phone.

His eyes grew wide as he read.

"What?"

He didn't answer her.

"What is it?" She looked at Dane, a sense of dread washing over her. Dane took several steps closer.

Blayze handed her the phone, his expression serious for once. She looked down at the screen and saw three Chattalot messages. The first one read, "Please, don't choose death." The second one said, "Choose life." And the third one said, "Your Father loves you." She slammed the phone down so hard that the table shook, sloshing her tea out of her glass. Your father? What did that mean? Why was the *f* in father capitalized? Did the writer mean God? No, of course not. That was just her guilty conscience talking. They meant her very earthly, very human father.

Dane was there in a second. "What is it?"

With a trembling hand, she handed him the phone.

He read the messages, looked around the room, and said, "I don't think there's an immediate threat. You enjoy your dinner. I'll call the police."

"No, don't," she hissed. "I don't want this getting out." She looked around the restaurant, but no one was paying any attention to them. Her heart was pounding, and she hated herself for it. This wasn't that big a deal. She shouldn't be so shaken up by some stupid social media messages. She snatched the phone out of his hands. "Thank you. You can go back to your corner now."

Pain danced across Dane's face, and she felt terrible for the way she'd spoken to him, but it was too late to take back the words. His expression returned to stoic, and he returned to his corner.

"Are you ready for that drink *now*?" Blayze asked, his voice so smug it made her thirsty.

# 32

Dane stood in the dark corner of the restaurant and tried to squash his emotional hurt. She had certainly put him in his place, hadn't she? And yet, he wasn't really mad at her. He was worried about her. He could tell that she was afraid, and that she didn't want to be afraid. This belief was affirmed when the server brought her a glass of wine. *Terrific. This evening just got worse.* He silently chided himself for the thought. Just because she'd drank too much champagne one night weeks ago didn't mean she would drink too much wine tonight. Maybe she'd just have a glass and be done with it. Dane did know that Blayze was happier when someone was drinking with him.

No matter how much time Dane spent with the guy, his opinion of him didn't improve.

Dane was itching to call the police, but he wanted to be able to show them the phone when he did so, and he couldn't get the phone away from his boss right now. He hoped the trail wasn't growing cold while Maggie and Blayze sat in the world's slowest restaurant drinking.

The food finally came, and Dane realized he was hungry. He'd grabbed a power bar before they'd left the bus, but that wasn't holding up now that he was surrounded by the smells of Alfredo sauce and steak, and now that he was literally watching Maggie eat. He flagged down a server and asked for a meal to go. Maggie had given him his first paycheck, so he could afford to eat now. He was proud of her. She was really doing it. She was touring on a bum ankle, the fans were loving it, they'd added dates to her tour, and her single had debuted at number ten. It was so smart of her to record that song, and he liked to think he'd played a small part in that. The fans loved her as wild child, sure, but they also loved the part of her that was a simple, down-home, southern girl.

When he returned his attention to Maggie, a new glass of wine had appeared. He groaned. She had a show the next night too. She didn't need a hangover, nor did she need to reinjure her ankle. She'd only just gotten off crutches, and now had a gompy walking cast to heave about, but it was better than the crutches. He didn't want her to have to go back to those things, and he knew she didn't want that either, but it wasn't his job to moderate her alcohol intake, so he bit his lip and stood in the corner, where she'd told him to stand.

With each glass of wine, it got harder for him to stand still, and he heaved a great sigh of relief when they both stood up from their seats before her fourth glass was finished. She wobbled a bit, but he thought that might have been from the ankle. She let out a soprano peal of laughter as she spun toward the exit. Blayze reached out to steady her, and Dane cringed at the fact that he was touching her. He headed toward the troublesome twosome in case they needed a grownup. Maggie continued to cackle as she staggered toward the door. Dane really wished her salad had been bigger ... or had more croutons ... or came with a side of bread—a *loaf* of bread. Dane reached her and then walked alongside them.

"Hang on a sec," he said to Blayze. "I've got to pick up a meal." He paid the woman at the busy cash register and then stood waiting for his food. What had he been thinking, ordering takeout from the slowest restaurant in the country?

"The cab's here, bud," Blayze said, making his irritation clear.

"He'll wait." Dane tried to sound firm. "It will only be a minute."

Blayze stood up straight and puffed out his chest. "You don't tell her to wait. You work for her."

"It's okay." Maggie patted Blayze on the chest. "We can wait. Why are you in such a hurry?"

Blayze gave her an irritated look. "I told you I wanted to go to that club."

"We'll go, we'll go, just wait for Dane. The guy's got to eat." She smiled at him then, and his heart swelled.

He decided he would just go without the food. Blayze had a point. Maggie shouldn't have to wait for his food, and he also needed to get her out of there. So he headed toward the door with his stomach grumbling.

A young woman chased after him. "Sir! You forgot your food!" She caught him and handed him a plastic bag tied at the top.

"Thank you," he said, and meant it a great deal. Carrying his delicious-smelling prize, he hurried to open the car door for Maggie. In the meantime, Blayze took the front seat.

"Hot Spot, on Second Street," Blayze said to the driver before Dane was even inside the car.

"Hang on a second, sir," Dane said to the driver, and then looked at the tired woman sitting beside him. "Where do you want to go, Maggie?"

"She wants to go to the club," Blayze said.

Dane ignored him.

Maggie looked at the back of Blayze's head. "I'm kinda tired. I think I just wanna go back to the bus."

Blayze turned around and glared at Dane. Dane wasn't the least bit intimidated by that glare. They'd gone about two miles when Maggie said, "I don't feel so good."

"Do you need to pull over?" Dane eyed her carefully.

Maggie seemed to think that over. "Nah, I just don't feel so good."

Dane wrestled with the plastic bag and then opened the Styrofoam container inside. He handed half of the sandwich over. "Here. Eat this."

"I already ate."

"You didn't eat nearly enough."

She took the sandwich out of his hands, and he licked some stray barbecue sauce off his thumb. Wow, that was delicious. He decided that this was the perfect time to eat the other half. Not terribly professional, not what he'd usually do, but, in the moment, it seemed appropriate.

"This is so good," Maggie said through a mouth full of food. And even though Dane hadn't cooked or prepared said food, her compliment made him quite pleased.

They got Blayze delivered to his own bus—he didn't want to go clubbing alone—which felt like a weight being lifted, and then the cab dropped them off at Maggie's bus. Maggie motioned toward the driver. "Can you pay him? I'll get you back."

Dane handed him some bills and then hurried to beat her to the bus. "Let me check it out first."

"It's been *locked*, Dane."

"I know, but I want to be careful." They both stepped inside, and then he left her standing just inside the door as he made his rounds, which took less than a minute. Nevertheless, she was almost asleep on her feet when he got back to her. "Come on," he said, putting her arm around his shoulders. "Let's get you to bed." He helped her hobble the length of the bus and then pulled back the covers for her.

She fell into bed and let out a little cry.

"You okay?" He thought about sitting on the edge of the bed, but hesitated.

She started to cry.

He sat down. Now he was wrestling with whether to wipe away her tears. He looked around for some tissues, but didn't see anything.

"I don't think Blayze likes me," she cried out.

What?! Seriously? What was he supposed to say to that? "Um ... I didn't realize you were that into him."

She laughed and flopped her arm over her teary eyes. "I'm not!"

Phew! "Then why are you crying that he doesn't like you?"

"Because no one likes me!" She was really crying.

He couldn't believe it. Had she lost her mind? He had no idea what to say to her. She was drunker than he'd thought she was. "Uh ... Maggie? Thousands of people like you. That's sort of why you're a star. That's what it *means* to be a star."

She laughed humorlessly. "That doesn't count. They don't really know me. I mean, I want them to like me, and I guess it sort of counts, but no one really knows me. They don't really know me. That's why they like me." She let out a giant sob, and he rubbed her arm, feeling helpless. How was he supposed to comfort her? This didn't even make any sense. "I just want to be liked." Her body shook with sobs. "All my life, all I've ever wanted was to *matter*. To matter to someone. But no one has *ever* liked me. Why, Dane? Why hasn't anyone ever liked me?"

He was just about to ask her if she wanted him to hold her when she said, "You can go. I'm falling asleep."

He stood and looked down at her for what felt like a long time, and then pulled the covers up over her and left.

Maggie Hammer was a mystery.

# 33

Maggie watched the world go by out her window, wishing she had something stronger than ibuprofen on the bus. It felt like a marching band was having practice inside her head, and she had a show to do in a few hours. She shouldn't have let Blayze talk her into drinking. Why had she done that? He was a bad influence on her. She was so thankful she hadn't fallen off any stages.

Dane slid into the seat facing her, wearing an expression that said he wanted to talk.

"I know, I know," she said, ashamed. "I shouldn't have gotten drunk. Thanks for not letting me go to the club."

"I didn't stop you from going." He pointed at her. "You did that."

She smiled. Was he trying to make her feel better? How sweet.

"How's the head?"

She leaned her forehead against the cool glass. "How do you think it is?"

He chuckled dryly. "You want some water?"

"I've already drunk several gallons of it."

"Good." There was a long, awkward pause, and Maggie wondered what he was up to. There was obviously more he wanted to say. Finally, he asked, "Do you remember going to bed last night? I mean, you said some stuff. Do you remember it?"

It all came crashing back then, and she let her head drop into her arms onto the table. "Oh my gosh, I do now," she said into the tabletop. It was fuzzy, but she remembered enough to be mortified. She was pretty sure she'd gone on and on about how no one liked her.

Dane touched her arm, and held it there until she looked up at him. "You know that people like you, right?"

was looking at right now. Maggie started to sing and dance, and their rapture intensified. Her ankle had gotten so much better, and though it was still a bit awkward, she could do quite a bit of prancing about with the cast. Still, the stage dancers joined her during the second song and added ample flair to the show. This stage was smaller than most that they played, and Maggie used every inch of it.

Dane felt like he was watching a really loud version of Simon says. When Maggie danced, the crowd danced. When Maggie settled down for her acoustic set, most of the crowd sat down and became quiet. And when Maggie began to sing "Long Hard Road," the crowd sang with her. They knew every word. Every mouth moved in unison. It was a beautiful sight.

Dane hadn't seen a negative word about Maggie in the press for weeks. It seemed Nashville and the entire country music nation was forgiving Maggie Hammer for the great sin of growing up and leaving the nest. If it wasn't for the weirdo still sending death threats, it would be easy to forget that all of that drama had even happened. The police sure were taking their time tracking those messages. Granted, he was sure they had plenty to do, but still. The not knowing was driving him mad.

Maggie finished her show with a wild rendition of "Wild Child" and then thanked everyone for coming. "I'll be backstage for the next hour or so, and would love to meet some of you." The crowd roared their appreciation of this complete lie, and Maggie gave them a dainty goodbye wave.

She gave Dane a tired smile as she brushed past him.

He pretended to cough and said, "liar" under his breath. Then he laughed so she would know he was just kidding.

She stopped and turned toward him. "No, I'm not lying. This won't be so bad. I do like meeting fans, of course. It's just so awkward. I don't know what to say and I don't know how to be cool, and I'm afraid they won't like me up close."

So they were here again. "Maggie, you could sneeze in their tea and they would like you."

She looked quizzical. "Dane, was that an Office reference?"

What? "What are you talking about?"

She giggled. "You just quoted a line from *The Office*."

"Do people sneeze in each other's tea on *The Office*? I've never seen it."

She giggled again and took him by the arm affectionately. "Come on, let's go meet some people, and you should really watch *The Office*."

With a sudden desire to marathon an old sitcom, Dane allowed himself to be led down a crowded hallway toward a table and chair. Dane wasn't sure what the chair was for. He didn't think Maggie would have much time for sitting. A line was already forming behind a red velvet rope. Maggie waved to them and took her seat behind the table. A man in a suit asked her if she was ready, and she gave a nod. Then one by one, teenage girls approached and asked Maggie to sign posters, CDs, and journals. And Maggie was incredibly gracious, asking each of them for their name and thanking them for coming. Most of them wanted selfies, and Maggie obliged over and over. Her Twitter feed was going to be loaded.

Dane was impressed. She was being really sweet, and he didn't know if she was performing, but either way, he could tell it meant a lot to these girls. They would probably remember this for the rest of their lives and be lifelong Maggie Hammer fans.

An older woman stepped up to the head of the line. She looked bedraggled, wearing a long dirty gray trench coat. She had long greasy gray hair and a few missing teeth. Still, Maggie shook her hand and gave her a big smile, treating her no differently than the others. "I'm Maggie."

"Dori."

"It's lovely to meet you, Dori. Did you want me to autograph something?"

Dori nodded and pulled open her trench coat to reveal a large turtle tucked inside. "I was wondering if you would sign Sheldon?"

The man operating the red velvet rope stepped forward to intercede, but Dane held up a hand to stop him. Dane crept a little closer, just in case, but he didn't think Maggie needed any help with this. The girls in line burst into giggles, and he hoped Dori didn't notice that.

"I would be honored to sign Sheldon!" Maggie said, and her voice and face didn't suggest anything different. "Are you sure it won't hurt him? I don't know if Sharpie ink is good for turtles."

"He'll be fine," Dori said as she held the turtle out toward Maggie. The turtle promptly pulled its head inside its shell. Dane couldn't blame him. He'd often wished he had a shell for that purpose.

Still smiling, Maggie put one hand on the turtle and wrote with the other, as she softly said, "Hi, Sheldon, nice to meet you."

When the autograph was finished, Dori smiled and tucked him back into her coat. Dane reasoned that there must have been a special turtle pocket sewn into the lining. "Can I take a picture with you?" Dori asked, pulling a large iPhone from a different pocket. *Wow, everybody has an iPhone.*

"Of course!" Maggie came around the table and put her arm around the woman, leaning toward her with a big smile. She posed for the photo, and then asked, "You don't want one with Sheldon in the picture?"

Dane couldn't believe his ears. Who was this woman?

Dori shook her head, a grave expression on her face. "No, Sheldon doesn't like having his picture taken."

It took all of Dane's self-control not to laugh at that. Maggie did give it a giggle, but only a little one. "I understand," she said, which Dane knew to be a total lie. Maggie Hammer loved having her picture taken.

# 35

Maggie dragged her tired body up the bus steps. Her ankle was throbbing. The door had barely shut behind them when Dane said, "You're amazing."

*What?* She turned to look at him. "Huh?"

He smiled. "Let me check things out." He brushed past her to go make sure no one had infiltrated the locked tour bus while they'd been gone. He returned twenty seconds later and said, "I just wanted to tell you that the whole turtle thing impressed me."

She frowned. "Why?"

He fell onto the couch with a chuckle.

She sat down beside him. "No, really. Tell me why." She really didn't understand what could have impressed him. It was just a turtle.

He leveled a gaze at her and then reached over and put his hand over hers. "Because, Maggie, you signed *a turtle*. And not only did you not *say* anything sarcastic, it appeared you weren't even *thinking* anything sarcastic." He shrugged. "I'm just amazed sometimes by how kind you are. And I wish the whole world knew how kind you are. But I'm afraid that most of them only see the ..." His voice trailed off as he searched for the words.

"The mean streak?" she offered.

He smiled and nodded, removing his hand from hers.

She wished he hadn't done that just yet, but it was probably inappropriate to hold hands with your bodyguard, even if you were sort of becoming friends. "I don't mean to be mean," she tried to explain. "It just happens. But it's not because I'm not kind." She knew she wasn't making any sense. "I think it's just that, I've been through so much, I'm determined not to let anybody get the best of me ever again. And well, the world is a pretty awful place, and I probably get defensive too easily." She didn't like thinking that, let alone admitting it out loud.

Dane looked contemplative. "That makes sense. Anyway, didn't mean to psychoanalyze you. I just wanted to tell you that the whole turtle thing really impressed me."

His praise warmed her like that first sip of wine, only better. "Thank you." *He likes me*, she thought. *Not in a creepy way or a romantic way, but he genuinely likes me. He knows me and he likes me.* She could hardly believe it.

Dane glanced toward the driver's seat. "Where's Rex? Shouldn't we be hitting the road?"

"Yeah, I'll text the other bus, tell him to hurry up."

Dane chuckled. "Well, you can use some of that turtle kindness on your driver too. In fact, you can bring him back on, let him sleep here. I haven't had a nightmare in weeks. I think all the action is tiring me out, and I'm too tired to dream." He chuckled again, but it sounded humorless.

She had asked the driver to sleep on the crew's bus, claiming she wanted more privacy. If she recanted that direction now, it would be even weirder. "Nah, he's fine right where he is."

"If you say so."

Her phone buzzed with a texted answer. Rex was on his way. "I'm glad you're not having nightmares anymore, though. That's awesome."

"Yeah, it really is. I'm only a little afraid to go to sleep now." He smiled. "Are you all set? I'm going to turn in."

She didn't want him to turn in. She wanted to keep talking to him. It was hard to wind down after a show. "I'm all set. But I don't think I can sleep yet. Want to make some popcorn and watch *The Office*?" He hesitated, and she was embarrassed that she had asked. "Never mind. You go ahead."

"No," he said quickly, "I would love to watch TV. I'm just not sure *The Office* and I are a good match. Isn't it just about a bunch of nerds sitting around an office acting stupid?"

She laughed. "They're not *all* nerds, and it's hilarious. If you can get through the first season, you'll be hooked."

His mouth dropped open. "I have to watch an entire *season?*"

She laughed again. Had she inhaled giggle gas? Or was she just flying high from all his praise? "I think it's only six episodes." She stood up. "Tell you what, I'm making popcorn. If you want some, you have to watch *The Office* with me. I'll be in my bedroom."

Feeling his eyes on her, she went to her room and slid the door shut. She needed to change into PJs before she dealt with melted butter. The dress she was in had cost a small fortune, and she still had to wear it another twenty times. She hurried though, before he could lose interest and fall asleep.

When she opened the door, he was standing beside the microwave. He too had changed, and looked scrumptious in his sweats and tight white T-shirt.

He looked her up and down. "Cute."

She didn't know if he meant her or the pink plaid pajamas, but she said, "Thank you," and yanked the popcorn out of his hand. "Give me that. You'll do it wrong."

He laughed. "And there it is. The mean streak."

# 36

Dane followed Maggie into her very small bus bedroom. Maggie slid the door shut behind him, and he wished she hadn't. He could only imagine what Rex was thinking. The bus swerved, and he lost his balance. He caught himself before falling onto Maggie, but just barely. "Sorry," he said, his lips inches from her face. Golly, this room was small.

"No problem." She climbed onto the bed, holding the popcorn up in the air with one hand.

There was no room to sit anywhere except on the bed. There was barely room to stand. Fearing that what he was about to do was unprofessional and wishing that he had another option, he sat on the foot of her unmade bed. He wished the bed was made. Somehow that would have made the whole scene less intimate.

She scooted up toward the pillows and then patted the spot beside her. "Come on, don't be shy. I'm not hitting on you. This is solely an attempt to recruit you to *The Office* fandom."

He did as she requested and tried to get comfortable—but not *too* comfortable. Watching TV behind a closed bedroom door was bad enough. Falling asleep there would be much worse. Dane had no doubt Rex would blab about such things. There are no secrets on the road.

*The Office* wasn't all Maggie had made it out to be. Dane worried that the jokes were going over his head. He found the whole thing pretty stupid, but Maggie found it hysterical, and he enjoyed the sound of her laughter. Her laughing voice was a lot like her singing voice—beautiful. He was also enjoying the popcorn, and when it was gone, he hurried to offer to make more. He really wanted to get away from her—not because he wasn't enjoying her company, but because he was enjoying it *too much*. He was having thoughts and feelings he wasn't supposed to be having about his boss, about his friend, about the woman who had finally started to open up to him. She trusted him.

"No thanks," she said to his popcorn offer. "I've still got to fit into that dress tomorrow night."

"Okay." He licked the butter off his fingers and was glad to see the credits roll. "I should hit the hay then." He started to scoot down the bed, but she grabbed his arms.

"Wait. One more episode, please? It gets better, I promise. Michael isn't nearly as obnoxious in the coming episodes."

Dane didn't even know which one Michael was, but he had a hard time saying no to Maggie, so he leaned back onto her multitudinous pillows. "Okay, one more, and then I really need to get some sleep." Though he hadn't had any nightmares for a while, he was still afraid of having them, and he'd still had trouble falling asleep every night. Dane didn't know how to relax. Even when he *did* sleep, it was with his muscles tense and ready for action. Yet here, beside Maggie, so warm, hearing her giggle and the hum of the tires beneath them, he felt a new calm settle over him, and his eyelids drooped. He tried not to fall asleep. *Just twenty more minutes*, he told himself.

But it was no use. He drifted off to the sound of Dwight Schrute's voice, and slept dreamlessly for several hours.

Then, all of a sudden, he was back in the fire, screaming at the person dragging him. He felt Maggie's arms go around him, squeezing him tightly. "Shh, it's okay, Dane, you're safe. You're on the bus."

Relieved to hear her words, to hear her voice, he started to sit up. "I should go to my rack."

She pulled him back down. "Stay. Go back to sleep. I've got you."

The truth was, he *was* incredibly comfortable, and her body against his magnified this comfort. He didn't want to move—ever. So, shushing the voice that was telling him to be professional, he lay back down and slid his hand under the pillow.

Maggie wrapped her arm around his waist and pressed her body against his. "Just let me hold you," she said sleepily. "It doesn't have to mean anything. I just want to hold you."

# 37

It was time for another date with Blayze. Maggie wished she was doing anything else: shoveling manure, cleaning toilets, breaking rocks in the hot sun. She had a night off in Alabama, and she wanted to spend it on her bus. She wouldn't let it show, and no one knew, but her ankle was killing her. It was getting better, but it was taking its sweet time, and she feared she was doing too much with it.

Vowing not to let herself be persuaded into drinking tonight, she stepped off the bus to find a smiling Blayze waiting for her. He was wearing a shirt and hat she hadn't seen before. He really was a looker. "You look nice. How much did that hat run you?"

"Oh, this old thing?" He tipped it to her. "Only five grand."

She coughed. "You can't be serious."

He laughed. "It costs money to look this good."

Her mind flashed to those childhood dinners that had consisted of potatoes. Only potatoes. He opened the taxi door for her, and she slid inside shaking her head. He'd spent five grand on a hat, but he would probably make her buy her own dinner. She couldn't see Dane's face in the front seat, but she could only imagine what he was thinking. She hoped that later he would provide commentary about a five-thousand dollar cowboy hat.

She was thankful that it was a short ride to the restaurant, and when they climbed out of the cab, she was less thankful that two photographers were there to blind them with their flashbulbs. "Did you call them?" she muttered to Blayze.

He gave her a mischievous look. "We're the hot couple, right?" He took her by the arm, and it took all of her willpower not to yank her arm out of his grubby hands. She hurried toward the door, suddenly ravenous. Dane beat her there and opened the door for them.

"Thank you," she said, and he playfully winked at her. She feared that wink would be the high point of her evening.

At first, the dinner was the same as it always was. Blayze drank a lot, tried to get her to drink a lot, and the salad was nothing to write home about. But then, when the server asked if they wanted dessert, Blayze said yes, a definite deviation from the course.

She looked at him suspiciously. "What's up?"

"Well, I was wondering ..."

*Uh-oh.*

"Are we really a thing?" His tone suggested that he thought this a profound question.

She hesitated. She wasn't in the mood for this conversation. "What are you asking me, exactly?"

"I mean, we've been seeing each other for a while now, but the relationship doesn't seem to be ... progressing."

*You've got to be kidding me.* "Yeah, so, I think that this relationship is mostly for show, right? I mean, I enjoy hanging out with you," she lied, "but I'm not looking for anything serious—"

His face registered horror. "I'm not looking for anything serious either. I just don't know if we're a real couple or not. I mean, I've tried to be patient, but it's been *weeks*."

She hated him. She leaned forward and gave him a playful smile, in case anyone was watching. "In no way, shape, or form," she said softly, "are we a real couple." Without meaning to, she glanced at Dane, who was, as always, faithfully standing in the shadows. She couldn't see his facial expression. This made her sad.

"What are you looking at him for?" Blayze snapped.

Oops. "Sorry, just making sure he was still there."

"Of course he's still there. He's *always there*." He leaned away from her abruptly. "You know what? I'm done!" He slammed both hands down on the table, clinking his empty beer bottles together. "I'm not playing your game anymore."

"Blayze, sit down," she said through clenched teeth, terrified he was going to expose her ruse. Everyone was staring at them. She was sure that not everyone knew who they were, but some probably did. Or would, before Blayze finished making a scene.

Out of the corner of her eye, she saw Dane tentatively approaching. She knew she didn't need him, but she appreciated him coming anyway.

Blayze somehow knew what she was really worried about. "Oh, don't worry. I won't tell them you're a fraud. I'll do you one better." He turned toward the other diners. "Sorry, for the interruption, everyone. I've just found out that my girlfriend, the *famous* Maggie Hammer, who sings songs about being a good old-fashioned down-home country girl"—*I don't sing songs like that!*—"is cheating on me with her gobydaurd!"

*What?* It took her a second to realize what he'd meant, and then she fought not to laugh at him. He really shouldn't have had that last beer if he was going to do some public speaking tonight. He waited, arms spread out to his sides, for a horrified gasp from his audience, but it didn't come. Most of them just looked confused. Then someone to the right snickered, and that snicker was contagious. It traveled across the room, slowly at first, and then picking up speed, until it hit Maggie, who couldn't resist its force.

Blayze turned and glared at her as the snicker traveled through her and continued around the room. "What? What is everyone laughing at?" When she didn't respond, he turned back to the others. "You chink cheating chis chunny?" he cried, arms outspread again. Whoa, that one was even worse. Was he okay? Maybe it wasn't the beer. Maybe he was having a stroke.

She stood up to go to him, just to check on him, but she'd only taken a few steps when he turned to her and pushed her in the chest so hard that she fell back into the booth, which, thankfully, provided a softer landing than the floor. Still, she managed to hit the side of her head on the table, and it hurt mightily. But she wasn't thinking about that. She was thinking about defending herself from further harm, and she sprang to her feet, ready to fight or run, whichever would be more efficient—but she didn't need to do either. As she stood up, she saw Dane going down, with Blayze beneath him. She couldn't imagine how Dane had gotten there so fast, but he had, and before she could say "boo," Dane's knee was in the center of Blayze's lower back, pinning him facedown to the floor with one arm twisted behind his back.

Blayze cussed and spat, wriggled and drove the silver toes of his cowboy boots into the floor, but it was to no avail. As Dane held his arm with one hand, he pulled out his cell with the other. She couldn't hear what he said into the phone—the diners were applauding too loudly—but she knew he was calling the police, and for once, she wasn't upset about that. He glanced at her as he spoke, and his eyes spoke volumes: apology, sadness, concern, and affection.

She, however, fell nothing. Complete numbness. She thought she should be angry or embarrassed, but she just stood there like a blob, incapable of forming a thought, of having an emotion. A server came to check on her, asked her if she needed anything, but she didn't even answer. She just stood there staring at the two men in her life, one of whom was about to leave it.

# 38

Dane never thought he'd be so relieved to step into the confines of Maggie's tour bus. Normally, he didn't like small spaces, but right now, it was paradise. It was the middle of the night, but he was wide awake. Maggie was abnormally calm, and this drove him crazy with worry. She'd spoken to the police, answered all of their questions without any snark, and then answered question after question from reporters who showed up like starving vultures to feast on her adversity.

He put his elbow against the wall of the bus and leaned on it.

She sat on the couch taking off her nylons, which was always a trick with her walking cast.

"You okay?"

"You've asked me that eighty million times, and the answer is always the same. I'm fine." With nylons removed, she leaned back on the couch cushions and closed her eyes. "I'm starving. Do we have any kettle cooked potato chips?"

He flipped open a cupboard. "We have regular potato chips. Sour cream and onion—"

"What kind of a monster put those in there? Seriously, we don't have any kettle cooked?"

He looked again, even though he knew there weren't any there. "No, sorry."

"I need a personal assistant. Someone I can send to the store in the middle of the night to get the correct potato chips."

"You're being a diva," he said, trying to be funny.

She glared at him. She didn't think he was funny.

He held up one hand. "Sorry, sorry. Just kidding." He went over and sat beside her, keeping a respectful distance.

"No, *I'm* sorry. I suppose I should thank you for your heroics."

He considered his words carefully. "For the record, I had no doubt you could take care of yourself. It's just that ... I've been wanting to slam that guy to the floor for months now."

She giggled, and it was such a beautiful sound that it made his heart soar.

"You really are okay, aren't you? I thought you were in shock or just pretending to be okay. You know, performing. But you're actually okay."

She gave him a small nod. "I really am. It's not like I cared about the man. My heart's not broken. We weren't really a couple. I knew he was a slimeball. I guess I'm mostly mad that he's off my tour. He was a handsome, talented slimeball that women loved to buy tickets to see. And I'm a little embarrassed, because of all people, I should've known. I should have seen it in him. I knew he was a slimeball, but I would've sworn he wouldn't have hurt me. And I'm a little relieved that he didn't hurt me worse. I'm glad I was never alone with him." She slid down the bench seat and leaned her head into Dane's chest, and the smell of her strawberry hair almost knocked him windless. This was a bad idea. He shouldn't be holding her. She was his boss. He was a professional. As if it had a mind of its own, his arm wrapped around her, and then his lips rebelled as well, kissing her on the top of her strawberry head. She nuzzled further into him. "I'm so tired."

"I can imagine. Let's get you to bed." His brain finally taking command, he stood up abruptly.

She looked up at him, her face registering surprise and confusion. "Yeah, okay." She stood more slowly.

"How's your ankle?" He was concerned, but mostly he was just trying to redirect the moment.

She looked down at it. "Surprisingly good." She smiled up at him, but her eyes were tired. "The ankle is the least of my worries. Don't forget we've got that radio show in the morning."

He had forgotten. "Don't you want to cancel that?"

She snickered humorlessly. "Are you kidding? This is the best publicity opportunity of my career." She patted him on the chest as she walked by him. "But don't worry, I won't let the conversation be all about tonight. I'm not going to turn into some victim. I'll keep him focused on the music."

He watched her walk away, watched the door slide closed behind her, changed into his pajamas, brushed his teeth, and then climbed into his rack. Then he stared at the bottom of the bunk above him until morning sunlight streamed through the bus's windows.

# 39

Maggie tried to look confident as she walked into the radio station. She carried a large paper cup of coffee, her second that morning. She'd asked the taxi driver to take her through the drive-through. Dane trailed wordlessly behind, but she could feel his vigilance. It made her feel as though she could relax, like she didn't have to be on alert—because he was.

A friendly receptionist greeted her and showed her into the studio, where she was introduced to the host of *The Morning Show*: Janessa Pierce. Maggie's stomach sank. For some reason, she'd thought her interviewer would be a man. Not that she had anything against women; she didn't, but they were much harder to manipulate.

Janessa warmly welcomed her, showed her to her chair and her headphones and then scurried around the studio being busy before settling into her own chair with a bright smile. Maggie put on her headphones and then took a long haul off her coffee. A long silence ensued as the two women waited for their cue. During that silence, Maggie's phone chirped. Oh great, another Chattalot message: "I heard what happened. Now do you understand?" What? What did that even mean? Who was this lunatic?

Janessa brought her back to the moment by speaking into her microphone, "We're back and live with the lovely Maggie Hammer, solo artist formerly of The Hammer Family." Maggie cringed. "Welcome to *The Morning Show*, Maggie. Thanks for coming to chat with us so early in the morning!" Janessa had a lovely voice; she was born to deejay.

Maggie tried to clear her head. "It's an honor to be here. Thanks for having me."

"I want to congratulate you on all the success you've been having, but I know our listeners want to me to cut right to current events. Can you tell us what happened last night?"

Maggie's mouth fell open. This wasn't how it was supposed to go. *She* was supposed to be able to control the interview, its direction and content. She forced a smile, knowing listeners would be able to hear it. "I'd rather talk about all the success I've been having."

Janessa gave her a charity giggle. "Of course, and we will, but your fans want to know that you're okay."

"I'm okay," she said quickly, but her voice cracked on the word "okay." Horrified, she fought for control, but her exhaustion was winning. Her throat swelled, and her eyes welled up with stupid, embarrassing tears. What was happening? Why was this happening? This couldn't be happening.

"You know what?" Janessa said, and the compassion in her voice surprised Maggie, who looked at her to see that her eyes were also brimming with tears. "We're going to cut to a quick commercial and then we'll be right back. Stay with us, y'all." She pulled half her headphones off and looked at Maggie. "I'm so sorry. I didn't mean to upset you. I can't imagine what you're going through right now. I can't even believe you're *here*. My producers made me do it. Please forgive me, I'm a huge fan."

Maggie tried to smile, but her lower lip trembled. "Thank you."

"Do you want to cancel?"

Maggie raised an eyebrow. "What would your producers say to that?"

She shrugged. "They'd probably fire me, but I want to fire myself right now for making Maggie Hammer cry."

Maggie took a deep breath. "They want transparency?"

Janessa looked thoughtful. "They want drama."

"Then let's give them some." She forced a smile.

Janessa returned her headphones to her ears and pressed a button. Maggie sneaked a look at Dane in the corner and thought he looked proud of her. But that sentiment didn't really make sense in this situation, so she figured she must be mistaken.

"And we're back with Maggie Hammer. Sorry about that, folks, but understandably, Maggie is a bit emotional this morning, and I just wanted to give her a second to collect herself. She may be a superstar, but she's also just a person with a heart, like the rest of us. So, Maggie, are you comfortable sharing with us about what happened last night?"

"Sure," Maggie said, her voice coming out strong and confident this time. "What happened last night was the result of me making a big mistake. But the thing is, I didn't know it was a mistake till it was too late. Last night, Blayze Balin had too much to drink at a restaurant and then pushed me, and I fell and hit my head on the table. It was assault, plain and simple, and he has been arrested. I am pressing charges."

Janessa tried to say something, but Maggie didn't let her.

"Blayze is a talented musician and singer, and I wouldn't want to do anything to jeopardize his career, but I'm also not going to lie to cover for him."

Janessa hesitated before speaking, which resulted in an awkward pause. Finally, she asked, "Was that the first time he assaulted you?"

Maggie nodded, but then realized her listeners couldn't hear her nod. "Yes. I would never stay with a man who hits women."

Janessa jerked back. "Okay ... well ... you have been very brave in all this. Do you have anything you'd like to say to any woman who might be struggling with domestic violence—"

"Get out. Get out right now. Don't make excuses for him. Be strong. Put your kids in the car. Put your dog in the car and drive away. If you think you have nowhere to go, you're wrong. Just get out and then take things one step at a time."

Again, Janessa appeared speechless. Her voice was born to deejay, but probably not to interview. "Thank you, Maggie." She sounded upset, and Maggie didn't know what she'd said wrong.

"Can we talk about my music now?"

Janessa's mouth smiled, but her eyes didn't. "Sure. Why did you decide to cover a Nitty Gritty Dirt Band song?"

"Ah, you mean 'Long Hard Road,'" Maggie said, in case the listeners couldn't connect the dots. "I'm a Nitty Gritty fanatic. And that is one of my favorite songs of theirs. I thought it described my childhood pretty well. We were always struggling to make ends meet, and I fought against that feeling of lack by pretending to be Lorrie Morgan."

Janessa perked up at the mention of Lorrie, Maggie belted out a line from "Something in Red," and Janessa's expression softened. But in a flash, it turned back to steel. "Is there any truth to what Blayze accused you of last night?"

Maggie flinched. She hadn't been expecting that. "Absolutely none. I would never cheat on anyone, and I am in no way involved with my bodyguard. We have a professional relationship. That's it. Blayze was drunk and babbling."

"All right. Y'all heard the inside scoop here on *The Morning Show* with Maggie Hammer. Let's get back to the music." She pressed a button and pushed the mic away from her face. "It's not always that easy, you know."

Maggie stood. "What's not easy?"

"Walking away. You just alienated any abused woman listening, and there were probably a pile of them. Make it sound like you can just drive away. It's not that simple. It's never that simple."

Maggie stared at her, unsure of what to say. She didn't realize that Dane had come alongside her until he had gently taken her by the arm. "Let's go, Maggie." And because she didn't know what else to do, Maggie followed him out the door.

# 40

D ane never grew tired of watching the show. Maggie pranced around, belting out her opening number, so comfortable now in the walking cast that he wondered if she'd be able to dance without it.

She finished the song, returned her mic to the stand and then stood there with her hands on her hips, waiting for the crowd to settle down. This was not in the script. What was she up to? She held her hands out and moved them down slowly. "Thanks for the support, y'all, but can we have a little chat?" They simmered down. "Then I'll get on with the music, I promise." A few stray cheers rang out from the nosebleed seats. "How many of you heard my radio interview this morning?"

From the sound of their response, many had. Dane couldn't *believe* she was bringing it up. He'd tried to get her to talk about it at several points throughout the day and she'd refused.

"Well, I'm afraid I owe some of you an apology. Please understand that I was so tired this morning I was running on coffee fumes." Some laughter spurred her on. "But I didn't mean to suggest that domestic violence is a simple issue with a simple solution." She took a deep breath, and then her voice softened. "Believe me, I know it's complicated. And I would never want to make a woman feel bad about the situation she's in. Because, it's never her fault. But this morning, I just wanted anyone listening to hear me say that there is hope." She stopped and then repeated herself for emphasis. "There is hope. You are not trapped. No matter your situation, you *can* leave. I know it's hard. I know it can seem hopeless, but it's not. Be strong. I know you've got it in you," she said softly. Then she took a step back and said with more gusto, "And I'm sorry, but I won't be singing any duets tonight." She motioned to her band, who fired up the next song. When she turned to look at them, Dane felt like she looked right at him, though it was doubtful that she could see him. He was standing in the darkest spot he could find, trying to be invisible.

His heart ached. He knew that nothing could ever happen between Maggie and him. He knew they could never be a couple. Yet it had hurt to hear her tell the deejay this morning that it wasn't possible. Why had it hurt so much? It didn't make sense. Sure, he liked her. Sure, he was attracted to her. But that's where it stopped. He wasn't foolish enough to fall in love with her, and he hadn't. He wouldn't. So why did his chest feel like it was being cracked open?

He watched her sing and dance and was so grateful not to have to hear her and Blayze sing their duet again. He'd heard that enough times for a lifetime. In fact, he hoped he'd never have to hear Blayze Balin sing again.

A stagehand came alongside him, which was weird. They never paid him any mind. He elbowed him in the side, and Dane resisted the urge to break his arm. Dane noticed a few other roadies standing in a cluster watching. So this guy had been egged on to come talk to him. Oh boy, this should be good.

"Is it true?"

At first, Dane didn't look at him. He just kept his eyes on the stage. If he were the only one involved in the scenario, his MO would have been to ignore the little creep entirely. But he wasn't the only one involved. Maggie was involved. Maggie's reputation was involved. So he looked down at the man and said, "Of course it's not true."

"Took you an awful long time to answer there, pal."

He did not respond to that.

But the urchin wouldn't go away. "You're the only one on the bus. You've even kicked the driver off. You really expect us to believe nothing's going on?"

Dane's neck was fiery hot. It took every ounce of self-control he'd ever had not to grab the guy by the throat and pin him to the wall.

Instead, he turned fully toward the man, who wisely took a step back, and said, loudly enough for the gaggle of onlookers to hear, "I am a war veteran with PTSD. I have nightmares that can be embarrassing. Maggie has created an environment that has afforded me the least embarrassment possible." Their faces fell, and the interrogator backed away slowly. "Is there anything else you would like to know?" They all turned away, and Dane turned back toward the stage, wishing he could spend some time with Maggie away from all the lights and people. But he knew that would never happen.

# 41

Maggie was halfway between Birmingham and Shreveport, and halfway through the third season of *The Office* when her phone rang. She was going to ignore it until she saw that it was the Nashville Police Department.

"Hello?"

"Hello. This is Officer MacKenzie with Nashville PD. Is this Maggie Hammer?"

"It is."

"Good afternoon, Ms. Hammer. I'm calling about your case. There's been an arrest."

Maggie sat bolt upright. "Who?"

"Elizabeth Wall-Wilcox. They've got her in custody in Tyler, Texas."

Maggie's stomach rolled, and sweat broke out on her brow. "There must be some mistake."

"Do you know her?"

"Yes, that's Bessie, my mother's friend. But she's my friend too, sort of. She wouldn't hurt me."

There was a small pause. "Ma'am, I'm sorry, but she's confessed."

Despite having a million questions, Maggie couldn't think of a single word to say. She thanked the officer and hung up. She had to get to Tyler. Would Bessie still be there when she got there? Yes, unless someone bailed her out. Maggie didn't think that was likely. Bessie didn't have any rich friends. Oh *wait*. She did now. She had The Hammer Family. She had to call her mother. She didn't want to, but she had to be a big girl and scroll through her contacts till she found the word "Mom."

Serena Hammer answered on the first ring. "I've been wanting to call you, but I didn't think you'd want to hear from me."

Maggie ignored all that. "Did you hear?"

"Of course I heard. It's all over the news."

It was? She hadn't heard a peep.

"Mom, I need you to not bail her out until I get there. I need to talk to her."

"What? Bail who out?"

Maggie rubbed her temple. "You just said you heard it on the news."

"I heard about you and Blayze. But you said bail *her* out. What woman got arrested?"

Maggie rolled her eyes. She was not going to talk about Blayze with her mother. "Bessie. Bessie is the one who sent the letters and messages. They've got her locked up in Tyler. But I'm on my way to see her." Maggie moved the curtain aside to look out the rear window. That wasn't quite true yet. She opened the door and made her way toward the front of the bus.

"What are you talking about? What messages?"

Oh shoot. She hadn't told her mother about her secret admirer. "Hang on, Mom." She tapped the driver in the shoulder. "We need to detour to Texas."

He laughed. "What?"

Maggie didn't think she'd said anything funny, and she didn't have time for banter with her driver. "Texas. Surely you've heard of it. I need to go to Tyler. It's just over the border. It will hardly be out of the way at all."

"Tyler is more than just over the border, and it will make us late for your show."

"Take me to Tyler or you're fired." She held the phone up to her ear. "Sorry, Mom—"

"Did you just fire your driver?" Her mother sounded horrified.

"Yes, and you should fire your driver too."

Dane appeared behind her and put a gentle hand on her shoulder. "What's going on?"

She took him by the other hand and led him to the couch, and they both sat down. "I'm sorry I didn't tell you sooner, Mom, but I've been getting weird letters. Threats. From someone angry at me for leaving the family. I thought it was some nut-job fan, but apparently, it was Bessie."

Her mom was silent for several seconds. "That's impossible."

"I know. I said the same thing. But they say she's confessed. Mom, I need to talk to her. I need to find out why she did it. And I figured she'd call you to bail her out, but please don't. I need her to be there when I get to Tyler."

Another long pause. Then, "Sorry, honey. I'm not leaving Bessie in a cell to wait for you. I don't believe she's done anything wrong. I don't know how they got her to confess to such a thing, but she didn't do it. I'll bail her out, and I'll make sure she's available to talk to you when you get there." There was another pause as Maggie considered whether it would be fruitful to argue with her. Her mother broke the silence. "I love you, honey. I'll see you soon." Then she was gone.

Maggie lowered the phone from her ear and looked up at Dane's wide eyes. "We're going to Texas."

"I heard that. We're going to Tyler? Isn't that fairly big? I thought you were from small-town Texas."

"I am. But we went to church in Tyler. Bessie's church. Drove twenty miles every Sunday, past twenty churches, just to get to one my father approved of." She stopped talking. Her brain was spinning.

"Did the police call you?"

She nodded. All she wanted to do was sink into that thick chest of his and stay there till Texas, but instead, she sat up straighter. "I don't understand it. It doesn't make any sense. Bessie wouldn't hurt me. Although. I guess she might be crazy enough to threaten me just to get me to go back to the family." She made a *pfft* sound. "As if that would ever happen. There aren't enough threats in the world."

# 42

Elizabeth (Bessie) Wall-Wilcox lived in the smallest house Dane had ever seen on a dead-end street at the edge of Tyler, Texas. Dane felt like he was walking around in a *Friday Night Lights* episode—except of course for the giant tour bus parked on the street at the end of Bessie's driveway.

At Maggie's knock, Serena Hammer opened the door.

"Is she here?" Maggie asked, and barely waited for the nod before pushing past her mother. Dane waited for Serena to step out of the way before entering. Before they had gotten off the bus, Dane had asked if Maggie wanted him to stay behind. Now that they knew, or at least were fairly certain, that Bessie was the threat, it didn't seem like there was much of a threat. But Maggie had told him she wanted no such thing, and so here he was trailing behind her down a stiflingly hot, dark hallway toward wherever Bessie was waiting.

The destination turned out to be a Formica-laden kitchen. Bessie sat at a table straight out of the 70s. He found a spot in the corner and tried to blend into the shadows.

Without invitation, Maggie sat down opposite Bessie, and reached out and took her hand. "Why?" she asked softly.

Bessie looked at the table.

"And how did you climb a fence?"

She looked at her then. "I didn't."

"How did you get to my door to tape a note up?"

She shrugged. "I hired a kid."

Maggie rolled her eyes. "I can't even believe you, Bessie."

"The police are saying they were death threats," Bessie hurried to say, her voice shaking, "but I didn't mean them that way. I was ... and am

... worried about where you are going to spend eternity. I was trying to get you to do the right thing." She looked over her shoulder at Serena, her eyes full of humility, and then back to Maggie. "I'm sorry if I scared you."

Maggie looked thoughtful. "What do you mean they weren't death threats?" Word by word, the softness was leaving Maggie's voice. "What else would you call them?"

Dane began to replay the text of each message in his mind. He had them all memorized. "Oh!" he said, and all three women turned to look at him. "Sorry, didn't mean to interrupt, Maggie. I was just thinking about the notes. They all suggested you were headed for some sort of punishment, but they never said Bessie was going to be the one to do it. Remember? She wrote that you'd regret your choices, that you'd face consequences." Suddenly, through this new lens, the threats all seemed innocuous, and Dane was embarrassed he hadn't seen them that way before. "Maybe she really was warning you of God's wrath or something."

Maggie slowly turned back toward Bessie. "You've got to be kidding."

Bessie shook her head. "I love you, child. I've loved you for your whole life. I don't regret trying to warn you away from your destructive ways, but I would never hurt you."

"You've got to be kidding," Maggie said again. She let go of Bessie's hand and leaned back in her chair, placing her hands in her lap. Dane could see that her fists were clenched. She was still furious, maybe even more so now. He wanted to go to her, to comfort her, but that was not his role here.

The silence stretched out until Serena broke it. "Surely, you can forgive her, Maggie."

Maggie glared at her mother. "Don't talk." Then she looked at Bessie. "I can forgive you, not because my mother tells me to, but because I know you're a good person and you wouldn't hurt me. I wish you hadn't done that. You scared me. I've been looking over my shoulder for months. I've had trouble sleeping. What did you think was going to happen? Did you think a few scary letters were going to change me? Don't you know me by now? Your little stunt forced me to hire a bodyguard, for crying out loud!"

Forced her? So she regretted hiring him? Wished she'd never had to? Dane tried to ignore the sickness that washed over him at that thought.

"I don't know what's going to happen, legally," Maggie said. "You sent these messages online, which I think makes them more serious." She looked as though she doubted herself. Dane didn't know how the law worked there either. "How do you even know about the Chattalot app? Do you even own a smartphone?"

"I used my granddaughter's," Bessie said, studying her own hands.

Maggie ran a hand through her hair. "Okay, I think I should go. I've got a show to get ready for." She reached across the table and took Bessie's hand again. "I will do everything in my power to keep you out of trouble, Bessie. But this was really, really stupid. And I don't know how much I can do."

"Maggie!" Serena scolded. "Be respectful."

Maggie let go of Bessie's hand and stood. "Whatever, Mom." She looked at Dane. "Let's go."

Dane motioned for her to go first down the hallway and then followed her. "Thank you!" Bessie called after them. Maggie lifted a hand in a wave without turning around, but Dane didn't even think Bessie could see that wave, which might've been a good thing, as it was dismissive and rude. But overall, he thought Maggie had been gracious. The woman had put her through an ordeal.

When they reached the door, Serena put a hand on his arm. "Could I have just a moment with my daughter?"

Dane looked at Maggie for a cue, and she gave him a nod that said it would be okay.

"I'll be just outside." He stepped out into the hot sun, and the screen door banged shut behind him. He took two steps to the ground and stopped to wait. He didn't mean to eavesdrop, but he could hear them clearly.

"Maggie, about Blayze, I'm so sorry." Her voice broke with tears. "I know that kids often follow their parents' examples—"

"Stop it, Mom. Stop right there. I wasn't even dating the man. I would never date a man named *Blayze*. It was just a publicity stunt. And that was the first time he ever touched me. I am not you. I will never be you. You don't have to waste one more second worrying about that." The screen door banged shut again and then she was standing beside him looking up at him impatiently. "Let's go!"

"Maggie," he said tentatively, knowing he was overstepping his boundaries. "You really want to leave things like that? You were so sweet with Bessie, but you can't extend that same mercy for your own mother?"

Maggie took three steps closer until she was right in front of him looking up into his face, her lips only inches from his. "You are my bodyguard, not my therapist."

With the threat gone, Dane wondered how much longer he would even be her bodyguard.

# 43

A week after her visit with Bessie, Maggie got a call from the DA's office. It sounded as though Bessie was going to get a plea deal and not do any jail time. This was a relief to Maggie. She was still furious with the woman, but she knew Bessie hadn't meant any harm.

Plus, she had other stuff to worry about. She needed to find another opening act. She needed to decide which song would be her next single. And she needed to decide if she still needed a bodyguard. Her heart cracked at the thought of letting Dane go, but did it make sense to keep him on? How would that look? Despite her constantly insisting that they were innocent, that nothing was going on between them, people were still talking about her and Dane. Did she, at this stage in her career, really need a personal bodyguard? Each day, she promised herself she would deal with it tomorrow.

About an hour before her show in Pigeon Forge, Oliver appeared. She was always happy to see him, and he being at her shows made her even more motivated than usual. She always gave her audience all she had, but knowing Oliver was watching put some extra pep in her step.

This time, Oliver wasn't smiling. He beckoned her into her dressing room. Dane gave her a raised eyebrow that asked if she wanted him to come along, and she gave him a nod that said she did. She and Dane hadn't talked much over the last week. He'd been fairly silent since she had snapped at him in Bessie's driveway. She missed the sound of his voice, but didn't know how to apologize. Maybe it was better for them if they weren't so close.

Dane closed the dressing room door, and Oliver took a deep breath. "I think you might want to cancel the show."

Maggie gasped. "What? Why? Is there a bomb?"

Oliver shook his head. "Your mom is in intensive care in Nashville."

Maggie's heart started to race, and she tried to control it. "Why? What happened?"

Oliver shrugged. "No one really knows. But it's serious. I just found out as I was pulling in here."

"What happened?" Maggie asked again through gritted teeth. "Tell me what you know."

"I don't know much. No one does. It appears she has been assaulted. Probably mugged. Someone dropped her off at the hospital. The police are investigating."

"Mugged?" Maggie shrieked. "She was most certainly not mugged! I know exactly what happened." She looked at Dane for guidance. She didn't know what to do. She was scared, and she didn't like that emotion, and she wasn't good at dealing with it.

"I know that you're tough, Maggie, but your reaction tells me that you need to get to her right now."

"You don't know anything about my reaction," she spat and then looked at Dane again. Why did she keep looking at him? What did she expect him to do? She wanted him to swoop in and be the voice of reason, to make everything all right, but she'd also made it clear that none of that was in his job description.

She tried to maintain her composure as she leveled a gaze at Oliver. "Not canceling the show. I'll go see her after."

Oliver reached out and took her hand. "Maggie, she might not last that long. I'm telling you, it's serious."

"And I'm telling you, I'm not canceling my show." She marched toward the door, and Dane looked as though he wanted to say something. Of course, he didn't. She had shut down that line of communication in Bessie's driveway. She turned and looked at Oliver. "Did you find me an opening act yet?"

"I'm working on it."

"Good." She stormed out of the dressing room and headed for the stage, but without permission, tears began to gush out of her eyes and she stopped and gripped the wall, trying to catch her breath. Of course, she couldn't, and she stood there panting, her tears splashing on the floor by her toes. Out of nowhere, thick arms wrapped around her waist and sweet lips pressed into the top of her head. He didn't say anything, and she appreciated that. What was there to say? Her father had probably finally killed her mother, and there wasn't a thing she could do about it. She certainly wasn't going to rearrange her life because of his evil. Not again. Not ever again.

# 44

As soon as Maggie walked out into the spotlight, Dane went to find Oliver. It wasn't difficult. He was on the other side of the stage, watching the show.

"Hey," Oliver said when he saw Dane. He returned his eyes to the stage. "She sure is something. Cold as ice."

"She's not, though," Dane said quickly, feeling defensive. "There's more to the story."

Oliver looked at him. "Do tell."

"I really can't." Dane racked his brain. What could he tell this man to make him understand that Maggie wasn't a cold-hearted monster, but not betray Maggie's trust? "Let's just say that her mother has been in danger for a long time, and Maggie's been warning her for a long time. So, she's worried about her mother, sure. And she's scared. I can see it in her eyes. But right now, she's mostly furious. Because all of this could have been avoided." He stopped. He'd probably already said too much.

Oliver stared at him, looking contemplative. "I see."

"Do you?"

Oliver looked at the stage and nodded. "I do. I really do. I'm sorry. I had no idea." He shook his head. "Wow, The Hammer Family. Isn't the husband the bus driver?"

Dane nodded, even though Oliver wasn't looking at him. He didn't dare speak again. He really had said too much.

"Wow, what a mess." He turned then and patted Dane's shoulder. "Thanks for telling me. I appreciate your trust." Then he vanished into the shadows of backstage.

Shoot. Maybe he shouldn't have told him. Maggie would be furious. But at least her manager didn't think she was a monster now. He watched the rest of the show, wishing it would last forever. He didn't want to have to face Maggie. He didn't want Maggie to have to face her worst nightmare.

But the show did end, and as soon as Maggie was changed, Dane led her back to her bus. A throng of people stood between them and it. So much for this venue's security. He stepped in front of her and held her hand, pulling her along behind him, keeping her as close to him as possible. "Excuse us ... thank you ... Ms. Hammer needs to get to her bus ..."

A particularly agile reporter slipped under his arm and stuck a recorder in Maggie's face. "Can you comment about your father's abuse?" Maggie didn't comment, but pressed herself into Dane's back. He kept moving, as another reporter shouted, "Are you going to see your mother?" Still another shouted, "Has your father been arrested?"

They reached the bus doors, and Dane pushed her through them before stepping on. As the door shut, she whirled to face him. "What was *that*?"

Dane looked at the driver. "Could we please get to Nashville ASAP? Maggie's mom's in the hospital."

"I heard, and yes."

"You heard?" Maggie cried. "How did you hear? What did you hear?"

"Oliver told me. He told me to get the bus fueled up and ready. And we're ready." He put his turn signal on and looked in his mirror.

Maggie went to the couch and collapsed. "How did those reporters know so much?" Maggie cried. "My mother's lived her whole life with that secret, and now she's going to die for it, and it won't matter, because everyone will know. The only thing she cared about was her family's image, and it's ruined." She sobbed into her hands. "It's all going to be for nothing!" She took off her high-heeled shoe and wound it at the other side of the bus and then she just screamed, a primal wail that made the hairs on Dane's neck stand up.

He sat beside her and put a hand on her back. He had to tell her. He didn't want to, but he had to. "Maggie, I'm sorry. I don't know how the reporters found out, but I talked to Oliver, and—"

She stood up and whirled to face him. "What did you do?"

"I didn't give him any details, but I didn't want him to think you were some cold-blooded monster who didn't care about your mother, so I just said a little, and well ... he figured out the rest." He paused and waited for the verbal lashing, but it didn't come. "But I doubt he told the reporters," he hurried to add. "I don't know how they found out."

Maggie looked toward the driver. "Stop the bus!"

"What?" Rex looked at her in the mirror.

"Stop the bus!" she screamed. Then she looked at Dane. "Get off my bus. You're fired."

His whole body went cold. This couldn't be happening. He held up both hands. "Maggie, please—"

"Get off my bus!" she screamed.

His heart was shattering into a million pieces, but he couldn't even be angry with her. He looked into her eyes and all he could see was pain. Years and years of it stacked up on one another. All those unanswered prayers. All those times she had begged her mother to run away, to get help. Now she thought she was going to lose her mother, and she felt helpless and furious. He knew she wasn't really mad at him. He was just the punching bag that was handy at the moment. "Okay, okay, I'll go. Can I get my stuff?"

She nodded, her lips pinched. The bus pulled over to the side of the road, and Dane hurried to fill his backpack. It didn't take long. He didn't own much stuff. He headed for the door but stopped when he reached her. "I love you, Maggie." He hadn't meant to say it. It just came out. "If you ever need anything, I'm here." He leaned toward her then, not knowing what she would do, and kissed her gently on the lips. He lingered there for a second, tasting her tears, feeling her body vibrate beneath his lips. Then he straightened and walked off her tour bus. He stepped back off the shoulder and looked up at the tinted windows. He couldn't see inside the bus, but he could feel her looking out at him. At first, the bus didn't move, and he thought maybe she was reconsidering. But then it pulled away, and he watched its taillights fade into the darkness, wondering if he'd done the right thing, and wondering if he'd ever see Maggie Hammer up close again.

# 45

Maggie missed Dane so much she felt like she had left part of herself standing behind on the side of the highway. She was ashamed of many things in her life but she had never made as bad a decision as that one. As the bus approached Nashville, she calmed down, recognizing that in that moment, she had been completely out of control. Oh how she wished she could take it back. But there was so much pain, so much anger, layers and layers of it etched in her soul. She couldn't imagine how she could begin to heal.

And then he had told her he loved her. What was that? As in loved her as a kindred soul? As an artist? A boss? A friend? Or did he mean that he *love* loved her? And if so, how was that even possible? She'd treated him like dirt, like less than dirt. She wished she could take it all back, but she didn't know how.

And so she was alone when she walked into the hospital to face her lifelong nightmare. She took the elevator to the ICU, and fought to keep the tears from falling, but it was a losing battle.

She stopped at the nurses' station and asked for her mother's room. Instead of answering, the nurse slipped her a handful of tissues and then asked another nurse for information. The second nurse gave Maggie a giant smile which at first infuriated her, but then the nurse spoke. "Your mother has been moved out of ICU. I can show you to her room."

Out of ICU? Did that mean she was going to live? "Is she going to be okay?"

"I'll let you speak to her doctor about that, but your mother is a strong woman." The nurse gave her another broad smile as she came around the counter. "I'm a big fan. Of hers. And of yours. Right this way." She led her back to the elevator, up to the next floor, and down the hall. Maggie didn't know what to think. Oliver had said that her mom might not make it through the night. So she'd let herself assume the worst. In fact, she had started grieving over an event that hadn't even happened and apparently might not happen. She stepped into her mother's room, and the nurse said, "I'll give you some privacy." The door clicked shut behind her, and Maggie looked at her mother, who looked so frail and small beneath the sheets.

"Hi, honey. I'm sorry."

Maggie hurried to her then. "Oh, Mom. You don't have anything to be sorry about. None of this is your fault." She kissed her on the cheek and gently pushed the bangs off her bruised and swollen face.

"I know it's not."

Maggie put her hand over her mother's, and Serena put her other hand over Maggie's and squeezed.

"On some level, I know that, honey. But you also tried to warn me, and I never thought it would come to this. I was wrong, and I'm so, so sorry."

Bawling, Maggie lowered her head to her mother's hands and rested her cheek on them. "Stop saying you're sorry. He did this, not you. You've just tried to be a faithful wife for your whole life." The relief gave way to anger and Maggie sat up again. "What set him off?"

"Evelyn has decided not to do another album with us at this time."

Maggie's breath caught. "So, I did this?"

Serena squeezed her hand again. "No, you did not do this. Truth be told, I only went along with this whole performing thing for you, because I knew you wanted it. But I didn't want you to leave us, because I wanted you by my side. I love you so much, honey. All these years, I've just been living for you kids, and I know I've hung on tighter than I should have. You've shown me that you are okay out on your own, and I know now that that's the way it's supposed to be. But that doesn't mean it's not hard on me." She swallowed hard. "I'm okay if this career is over.

I miss my calm, boring life." She chuckled. "Maybe we can do a concert every now and again, but I look forward to slowing down."

Maggie couldn't believe her ears. Why would anyone want to stop this life? "Are you sure?"

Serena nodded. "You are not me, and I am not you. We don't have the same dreams, and I know now that that's okay." She looked around the room. "Lying around here has given me some time to think."

The two women sat there for several minutes, silently crying, Maggie had never been so relieved in her whole life. She could feel some of those layers healing as she sat there. "Maybe we could do a duet sometime?"

Serena smiled through her tears. "Maybe we could, as long as I don't have to go on tour with you."

Maggie giggled. "I'll cancel my next few shows. I just want to spend some time with you."

"That is music to my ears, honey. But I do want you to leave my side to do one thing for me."

Maggie would do anything for her mother. "What's that?"

"You love him, don't you?"

Maggie knew exactly who she was talking about but pretended she didn't. "Love who?"

Serena shook her head. "Don't try to lie to me. I'm your mother. You love your bodyguard."

"I fired my bodyguard." Maggie's voice cracked on the word *bodyguard*. "Now that we know it was Bessie sending those messages, I didn't need him anymore." She didn't need to tell her mother the exact circumstances under which she had fired Dane.

Serena shook her head. "Good. I'm glad you fired him, because he shouldn't be your bodyguard. He should be your husband."

Maggie sat up straighter. "What? I don't want a husband!"

"I know you don't. You've been saying that your whole life. Because you grew up with your father and me. But I'm telling you that love is possible. Romance is possible. Happiness is possible. God wants what's best for you. Don't cut off his blessing because of what you saw in your parents." Serena's tears began to fall more abundantly. "Please, Maggie. You have a chance at a love I never had a chance at. Please don't let it go."

# 46

D ane's heart leapt when Maggie's name appeared on the screen of his phone. He couldn't answer fast enough. "How's your mother?" He had seen in the news that she was going to pull through, but he wanted Maggie to know that he cared.

"She's doing great, actually. I've been with her right steady. Even canceled a few shows, so now Oliver knows that I'm not a cold-blooded monster."

Was she trying to be funny? Trying to repair a small portion of the bridge she'd blown up with dynamite?

"Dane, I owe you an apology. I'm so sorry. I was totally freaking out. I didn't even know what I was saying, and I took it out on you because you were safe. I will understand if you can never forgive me, but I'm hoping you'll come back to work for me. I'll even count this as paid vacation."

As if he was worried about the money. "Maggie, I forgave you the second it happened. I get it. And I would love to come back to work for you. Where are you?"

"My next show is in Tampa. In three days. And we've even got an opening act, someone I've never heard of." She giggled. Oh, how he had missed the sound of that giggle.

More than anything, he wanted to go back to work for her. To seeing her day in and day out, to watching her dance and hearing her sing. But a small voice in his head told him this wasn't a good idea. He'd declared his love for her. However clumsily it had happened, it had still happened, and she was pretending that it didn't. She was asking him to come back to *work*. That was it. Was it fair to him? To live with a woman who didn't return his feelings? He would *never* find love if he spent his life drooling after Maggie Hammer. And didn't he want to find love, eventually? And was it fair to her? Didn't she deserve to have a bodyguard who wasn't in love with her? A real professional?

"Dane? You're not saying anything."

He chuckled awkwardly. "Sorry, just thinking."

"And?"

Gosh, she could be so pushy. "And I'm wondering if me going back to work for you is the wisest thing. Maybe you should start fresh, with a different bodyguard."

"I don't want a *different* bodyguard. I want *you*." Even though the words made his heart soar, he knew she didn't mean them the way he needed her to.

"I don't know, Maggie—"

"I'll double your pay. I'm actually making money now." She laughed. "Most of it goes straight to Sequin's pockets, but I am in the black at least. I'm not totally broke anymore. Please, Dane?"

It wasn't the money that convinced him. It was the please. He couldn't say no to her. And if he was honest with himself, he didn't want to. He silenced that voice that told him this wasn't wise and said, "Sure. Can I hitch a ride to Tampa?"

She laughed. "Yay! Thank you, Dane! I'll make it up to you. All of it. I don't know how yet, but I *will* make it up to you."

He knew exactly how she could make it up to him—by returning his feelings. Was he crazy? Was she really that out of his league? Hadn't he sensed that she cared about him? Hadn't she kissed him first? Hadn't she returned his kiss when he'd kissed her?

Then he remembered Blayze, the man she'd pretended to date solely for the purpose of forwarding her career. If she *did* have feelings for her bodyguard, maybe she'd hide them because they wouldn't be good for her image. Or maybe a woman that concerned with her image would never have feelings for a guy like Dane in the first place. He just didn't know.

He tried to simplify it. Either she loved him or she didn't. If she didn't, then fine. That was the end of it, and he would just be her bodyguard. But if she did, well then, he just had to convince her that love was more important than her brand.

Piece of cake.

Maybe.

"You're being all creepy and silent again."

Dane laughed. "Sorry. Text me the details of where and when to catch the bus, and I'll be there."

"Thanks, Dane. You're the best."

He hung up the phone, fervently hoping that she'd meant that.

# 47

While Maggie was still in Nashville, Oliver got her a gig at Wildhorse Saloon. They'd had a last-minute cancellation, and Oliver had pulled strings. Every day, she was increasingly more grateful for Oliver, who swore up and down he hadn't leaked information about her family to the press. And he promised that he never would. This made it even more awful that she'd kicked Dane off her tour bus in the middle of the night, but, she reminded herself, he had forgiven her, so she needed to let it go.

When she had called Dane, she had intended to tell him how she felt, or at least try to. She didn't even really understand how she felt. But she knew that there was something special there, something she'd never felt before. How could she be in love with Dane Longley if she didn't believe in love? She had no idea, but that didn't mean it wasn't happening.

But she'd chickened out. She'd talked about the *job* instead of telling him the truth, no matter how messy that truth was. She liked to think she was tough, but in this case, she was a complete chicken.

It was her first show without the cast, and she was thrilled. She felt so much lighter. The Wildhorse was packed, and she was so grateful for the audience's visible and audible support. It felt like they were giving her one giant hug. The show grew so intimate that, before she sang "Long Hard Road," she had to say something about her mother. It felt dishonest not to. So, she waited for the applause to die down, and then she said, "I'm sure that most of you have heard about my family by now. It's been hard not to." There were a few polite laughs. "It is true that my mother has been a victim of domestic abuse for years. She tried to be strong for her children, tried to stand by her man, and tried to keep everyone believing that our family was happy and wholesome. Obviously, this was not the case. Still, my mom is a strong and beautiful woman, and I'm so thankful that she is all right, and my father will not be able to hurt her anymore. I'd like to dedicate this song to her."

She sang "Long Hard Road" like she had never sung it before, from the very depths of her being. She felt like she was giving the performance of a lifetime, and when she was finished, the audience's applause confirmed that notion. She wished Rodney Crowell had been there to see it.

It was hard to follow that performance, but she tried with her other songs, and the energy in the room slowly wound down until she finished off with "Wild Child." Then she thanked them all for coming and headed backstage.

As she walked into the shadows, she missed Dane mightily. He was always there waiting for her, like a big, giant, handsome rock that smelled like Christmas, and she couldn't wait till he was back at his post. Oliver met her instead with a big hug. A pretty young woman stood beside him. "Maggie, I'd like you to meet someone. This is Hannah Carter."

Maggie extended her hand. "Any relation to the Carter Family?"

Hannah laughed as she accepted Maggie's hand. "I wish."

"Nice to meet you." She looked at Oliver. Why was he introducing her to this woman?

"Hannah just started working for Platinum Publishing." Maggie had heard of it, a boutique publishing company in Nashville. It was small, but she'd been hearing about them more and more lately. Apparently, the woman who ran it really knew what she was doing, had an ear for the hits before they were hits.

"Congratulations," Maggie said. "Are you new to Nashville?"

Hannah's head pumped up and down. "From Maine originally. Anyway, I just wanted to tell you, so I asked Oliver to introduce me, because I wanted to tell you ..." She giggled nervously. "I'm sorry, I'm babbling. I'm a bit star-struck."

Maggie liked her. She liked people who liked her first. "Don't worry about it."

Hannah gulped in some air. "I wanted to tell you how inspiring you've been when you've spoken about domestic violence. And I have a song I think you might like." She handed Maggie a CD. "I really hope you like it. Thanks for meeting me." She turned and scurried off.

Maggie raised an eyebrow at Oliver. "Personal friend of yours?"

"No, and I usually screen you from these offers, but I've heard that song, and I think you should record it."

She looked down at the CD in her hands. "Really?"

Oliver nodded, looking grave. "Listen to it. If you can't turn that into a number one hit, I'll eat my hat."

Maggie, excited to listen to the song, hurried back to her condo, which felt empty and lonely without Dane. She got comfy on the couch and then pressed play, and it didn't take long for the tears to start flowing. Hannah's voice was beautiful, a soft, haunting soprano, but her words were even more powerful than her voice. "Sister, wherever you are, hear me plead with you. Sister, whoever you are, there's something you need to do. Don't just sit there and wait for change. Don't let him hurt you while you wait for change. Don't wait, don't wait, don't wait for something to change. Be the change, be brave." Hannah's voice exploded on the word brave and made the word travel over ten different notes before taking a breath. "Be brave! Please, sister, for the sake of your soul, for the sake of your heart, for the sake of your life, be brave."

The tears flowed down Maggie's face and soaked her hands, which were folded in front of her. Oliver was right. This would be a hit. She texted him, "Tell Hannah I'll cut it," and then listened to it again. She had gotten up on stage and told hundreds of women to be brave. She had said the same thing to thousands of women on the radio. But she, Maggie Hammer, wasn't even brave enough to tell a man how she felt about him. How could she sing this song, when she herself was a coward? She couldn't. And she wanted to sing the song. Which meant she couldn't be a coward. She had to go see Dane. She had to be brave.

# 48

A knock sounded on Dane's motel door. He hadn't gotten his own place yet. He hadn't been sure he was going to stick around Nashville, and then he'd gotten Maggie's phone call, so he was just killing time until he made his home on her tour bus again.

Still, he hadn't told anyone he knew where he was living, and he couldn't imagine who was at his door.

He peeked through the peephole to see Maggie's tear-streaked face. Her eye makeup was a fright. Oh yeah, he had told her where he was, in a text message. He ripped the door open. "What's wrong?"

She fell into his chest and wrapped her arms around his waist, and he was overcome by the smell of strawberries. He wrapped his arm around her and pulled her inside, fearing the worst. He closed the door with his other arm and then sat on the bed and pulled her down beside him. "What happened?" Had her mother died? Had she made some new, career-shattering mistake?

She pulled away from and tried to smile through her tears, but it came out strained and crooked. "Nothing's wrong, actually. Sorry." She wiped at her eyes and took a deep, shaky breath. "Dane, I know this will come as no surprise to you, but I'm not good with emotional stuff."

He laughed and then felt guilty for it. "I don't think many people are."

She rolled her eyes. "You're just saying that to make me feel better."

"Maybe." He laughed. She was right. Maybe loads of people were good at emotions. The poets and painters. He certainly wasn't.

She didn't say anything. She just sat there. But at least she had stopped crying.

"Are you hungry? Thirsty?" He was desperate to make her feel better.

She looked surprised. "Actually, I'm starving. You want to get something to eat?"

"Sure. Let's order in, given the condition of your makeup."

She moaned, and her cheeks got pink. He reached over and took her hand. "No, I wasn't being critical. I just know you worry about your image. You're perfectly beautiful no matter what the state of your makeup."

The tears started flowing again. "And that's why I'm here. Dane, I'm such a fool."

His heart started to flutter. What was happening here? Dare he hope? "Don't talk about yourself like that."

She looked around the room. "Will you order some food? Give me a chance to collect myself? My treat. Whatever you want." She turned toward the bathroom, but then turned back. "But nothing healthy." Then she went into the bathroom and closed the door.

He had this bizarre fear she wasn't going to come back out. He dialed the number to the Thai restaurant that had delivered his previous two dinners, and ordered two meals. Was Thai food too healthy? He ordered a side of crab rangoons as well. He didn't think those could be very good for you. Then he went to knock on the bathroom door.

She opened the door immediately and stepped out into his arms. "Dane, dear, sweet, Dane, I have to talk to you about something, and I fear I'm going to murder it. So, please be patient with me." He didn't know what she was going to say. He had hopes, but he didn't know. Still, he knew that he would wait forever to hear her say she loved him.

"When you kissed me on my bus, after I made the biggest mistake of my life, I felt something deep inside. Like, inside my soul, not just my body. Something changed in me in that moment, and I don't understand it. I have spent my whole life not believing in love. I've always thought it was just some chemical attraction that ended in babies and a train wreck." He held back a snicker. He didn't want to interrupt her.

"But you've changed my mind, sort of. I don't understand it. I have trouble believing it's real, but, Dane Longley, I don't want you to be my bodyguard anymore, because I'm in love with you."

There it was. He hadn't had to convince her of anything. Or maybe he'd already convinced her a long time ago. He placed his hand on the back of her neck and gently pulled her toward him, tilting his head to the side, and pressed his lips to hers. He pulled her body into his and tried to convey everything he was feeling with that kiss. Much to his delight, she deepened the kiss, and his head spun. How had he waited so long to kiss her like this? He didn't know, but it was worth every second of the wait. And somehow, despite all he had been through, despite all the fear and pain he still carried around with him, he knew that in the arms of Maggie Hammer, everything would be okay.

# 49

M en *shouldn't be allowed to kiss like this*, Maggie thought as she fought to keep her feet beneath her. A voice in her head told her to push him away, that this was dangerous, that she was setting herself up for pain and failure, but another part of her told that annoying voice to shut up. Kissing Dane felt too good, felt too right, and she didn't want to stop. She wanted to never stop. Kissing Dane made her believe in every love song she'd ever sung and made her want to sing more.

Then, much to her dismay, he pulled away. And he gazed down at her, his eyes tender, and his lips pink from her kiss. He caressed her cheek, sending shivers all the way down to her toes. "I love you too, Maggie Hammer. So, so much. I think I loved you the first time I saw you. I just didn't know it then. But slowly, the love has grown and grown until I thought my chest might burst from it."

She leaned into him and his fir tree smell and kissed his chest through his T-shirt. Then she nuzzled into him. "I hope not. I really like your chest."

He laughed, the sound of it vibrating through her face, and said, "Come on, let's sit down." He took her hand and drew her down to the bed again. "You look really good without the cast, by the way."

She laughed. "Thank you."

He traced the lines of her hand with his finger. "So, what does this mean? You're firing me again?"

She giggled. "Sort of? I don't know. I want you by my side, but I don't want to be your boss." She looked up into his eyes. "Does that make sense?"

He nodded. "Yeah, it does. Though I'm not sure my manhood can survive having a sugar mama. I do need a job. Could I be your bodyguard *and* your man?"

She nodded, only a little embarrassed of her own enthusiasm. "Does that work for you?"

He kissed her on the forehead and ran a hand through her hair. "Maggie, you have made me so happy. Yes, of course that works for me. And does it work for you to have everyone know you're dating your bodyguard? I mean, that's not going to do much for your image."

"Oh image schmimage," she said quickly. "Are you kidding? My image is a mess. The whole world knows I come from the most dysfunctional family in the history of country music—"

"I doubt that," he interjected.

"Okay, maybe you're right." She giggled. "But still, pretty dysfunctional. And I've made scene after scene in public, done a whole tour with a cast on, embarrassed myself by dating Blayze Balin." She smiled at him. "Obviously, I've been too worried about image. I just really wanted to make it in this business, but that seems less important now." She took a deep breath, trying to maintain at least a little control over her emotions, although, the more time she spent with Dane, the safer she felt. "I can't believe you even want me with this image of mine attached."

He squeezed her shoulder. "Oh, I definitely want you." He kissed her again, too briefly. "And *I* know that you are not your image. You are a real person, a person who is sweet and kind to people when they need it, a person who loves music so much that it makes me love music more, a person who makes me smile every single day—even when you are throwing shoes."

She laughed again and leaned into him. "I'm sorry it took me so long to tell you how I feel."

"The timing is perfect. You're perfect, Maggie. Just the way you are."

She knew that wasn't true. She was *far* from perfect, but knowing that he felt that way about her made her heart soar. Maybe she really could just be herself. She'd never tried that, at least, not that she could remember. Maybe she could stop fighting so hard to make people like her and just let Dane love her. Suddenly, she knew that, no matter what happened with her career, that would be enough.

# Epilogue

Hannah stood in the crowd looking up at the couple on the small stage. Maggie Hammer had invited *her*, Hannah Carter, to her engagement party. True, Maggie Hammer threw a party for everything, as often as she could, and true, she had invited half of Nashville, but still, Hannah felt pretty special.

Maggie had recorded her song, and it was climbing the charts, just like she'd hoped it would. So, wearing this fancy dress and drinking this fancy drink out of this fancy glass, Hannah felt like all her dreams were coming true. She should be completely happy and content, so why wasn't she? Why did she get this awful gut-wrenching feeling when she watched Maggie and Dane up there on stage, so happy together? Why did their joy make Hannah feel like she was missing some crucial part of living?

With one arm around Dane's waist, Maggie stepped up to the microphone and said, "Thank you all for coming. It's an honor to have you here and to announce my engagement to this wonderful man here. He's not much for public speaking, but that's okay, because I love microphones."

Hannah joined the crowd in laughing at that.

"But seriously, for a long time, I didn't even really believe in love." She smiled up at her fiancé. "All that changed when I met Dane." Then she smiled at the audience. "So, if you're here tonight and you haven't found your special someone, keep looking. Love is real, romance is real, and your person is out there. Don't give up. Keep singing the love songs, and keep believing." Hannah felt like Maggie was looking right at her. "You're happily ever after is just around the corner."

Hannah forced a smile. She was a huge Maggie Hammer fan, and Maggie had spoken lovely words, but Hannah didn't believe a one of them.

Check out Hannah's story in *The Songwriter's Rival*

# More Books by Penelope Spark

**Sweet Country Music Romance**
The Rising Star's Fake Girlfriend
The Songwriter's Rival

**Clean Billionaire Romance**
The Billionaire's Cure
The Billionaire's Secret Shoes
The Billionaire's Blizzard
The Billionaire's Chauffeuress
The Billionaire's Christmas

**Penelope also writes as Robin Merrill:**
Shelter Trilogy
Piercehaven Trilogy
Gertrude, Gumshoe Cozy Mystery Series
Wing and a Prayer Mysteries
And more!

www.ingramcontent.com/pod-product-compliance
Lightning Source LLC
Chambersburg PA
CBHW022108170626
46808CB00002B/657